THE BUTTERFLY AND THE SEA DRAGON
A YOELIN THIBBONY RESCUE

By Tyree Campbell

The Butterfly and the Sea Dragon
A Yoelin Thibbony Rescue
By Tyree Campbell

Cover illustration copyright 2016 by Laura Givens
Cover design by Laura Givens

First printing May 2016

Nomadic Delirium Press
Aurora, Colorado
http://www.nomadicdeliriumpress.com

For my sister Georgia,
who loved Nyx and would have loved Yoelin.
R.I.P. . . .

001

Entry into the estate house had offered but moderate security impediments for the tall woman named Yoelin Thibbony. Encased in black vivar skin, she padded lithely along the darkened hallway that led to the study. She kept to the right wall; the house schematics had indicated four statues on stands along the left wall. The NV goggles allowed her to pick them out one by one as she passed, although they barely showed up against the general background of the hallway. In the goggles, a green line along the bottom of the study door grew brighter as she approached. Now she tensed; the intrusion had transpired easily so far, a sure sign that the unexpected lurked ahead.

When it came, it almost made her laugh. On one step, her sprayshoe-clad foot pushed off against plush carpeting; on the next, the arch of her other foot pressed against something sharp and hard, and she fought the urge to cry out. She paused, took her weight off that foot, and located and picked up the offending object with her toes, transferring it to her free hand. Through the microthin layer of black vivar that covered her fingers she tested the shape of it . . . and stifled a burst of mirth. It was a piece from a child's toy, a plastic building block, a *Lego*, of the type found on the floors of homes with children on every world of Corporatia. They never picked up all the blocks, ever. On this occasion the *Lego* served as a reminder that there were other people in the house, and that she would prefer to avoid them if at all possible.

The woman slid the NV goggles up over her forehead. The line of light under the door to the study, now a mere three paces away, caused barely a ripple in the darkness, although it had been a beacon in the goggles. Her left thumb ticked at the Palmetto in her hand. The reading indicated one person in the study, and his heartbeat rhythms matched the EKG on record for Gunther Middenhill.

She moved to the door, and aimed the Palmetto at the touchpad on the wall beside the jamb. In less than a second she received the entry code: a pedestrian 4321. A tick to the Palmetto entered the code, and the door slid open as she slipped the device into a hip pocket.

The man seated at the desk rotated his floating chair to face her, but he withheld his outcry of alarm when he saw the finger pressed across her lips for silence and the Kreisler Energo in her left hand. As the door snicked shut behind her, she scanned the study, though she already knew the contents by heart. No windows. Three classic oil paintings, two on the back wall, one on the right. The three shelves of a wrought iron *etager* in the corner bore ancient bric-a-brac. Against the left wall stood an antique oak rolltop desk with artstate trappings, including a multifaceted monitor above the desk. From her oblique angle of vision she could just see that the upper left quadrant of the monitor contained text—a report in preparation, possibly, or diary notes. The chair hovered two centimeters above the carpet. Middenhill's left hand rested over the chair arm, over the controls there. As yet he had not moved his fingers.

Middenhill matched the hologram she had filched from official records. Several centimeters shorter than her meter eighty-three and paunchy, with a round head, brown eyes, and a pasty tan acquired under a sun lamp. His after-hours casual wear suggested his favorite color was turquoise green, although it did not go well with his tan or his eyes. He had thick arms that were just too short for his body, and facial skin that, at his age of hundred and twenty-two, had twice undergone retrotherapy, although he could still smile. Or frown, as he was frowning now.

Yoelin spoke through the opaque vivar that covered her head like a second skin, in English, in a smoky contralto that might have buckled the knees of an ardent admirer. "I'll have the cameo opal pendant in the silver setting, on its silver necklace."

Middenhill stared at her, his mouth open. "What?"

"I'd rather you didn't tap your fingers on the control panel on that chair arm, Mr. Middenhill," she said, and fired a yellow laser beam at his lower left leg, just searing the fabric there and the skin beneath it. Middenhill cried out, and stopped when he saw the Energo aimed directly at his nose. "I know it hurts," Yoelin said softly. "I know you have no security personnel on the estate, so there is no one nearby for you to summon. I know the control panel can alert security authorities in Port of Burkee, but by the time they arrive, which would be ten minutes from now, you would be dead, and I would have the pendant. I know the panel can also awaken the other members of your family, but that would only result in their quite unnecessary deaths." She paused, and added, "The pendant?"

"It-it belonged to my ex-wife," he argued. "It was part of the divorce settlement. It's not worth anything."

"I am fully aware of its history, sir. But that history is irrelevant to my contract, to this Rescue."

"Res-rescue? I don't understand."

She smiled without mirth. "That's what I do, sir. I rescue people, and things. In this case, the pendant. I'd like it now, sir."

"I . . . I have to go get it," he said. Beads of sweat popped through tightened pores on the retrofitted skin of his forehead. "It's—.""

"You keep it in the pencil slot in your center desk drawer, sir."

The air seemed to go out of Middenhill. With a heavy sigh he drew open the center drawer, and peered down at the contents. After a moment, he reached in and fingered the necklace, and finally held it up so that the pendant dangled at eye level.

"Place it on the corner of the desk, and ease your chair back," Yoelin ordered.

Reluctantly Middenhill complied. "I'll get it back," he said, defiance in his tone.

Yoelin picked up the pendant and necklace and tucked them into a pouch on her left thigh, then drew a fingertip across the top of the pouch, sealing it shut. "Mr. Middenhill," she said, her voice soft again, "even to attempt to retrieve this item will activate the other part of my contract, which stipulates that I am to kill you if you bother Elaine again."

"I'll double whatever she's paying you," blurted Middenhill. "Triple it, even."

Yoelin shrugged. "I get ten thousand thalers for the pendant," she replied. "Fifty thousand more plus expenses if the second part of the contract should be activated."

Middenhill's brow furrowed. "But . . . but the pendant isn't worth more than a hundred thalers."

Under the vivar, Yoelin smiled sweetly. "Heirlooms usually are over-valued by their owners. But that is not relevant to my contract." She withdrew the Palmetto and rekeyed the door code, stepping to one side while it opened in order to avoid surprises. Light from the study reached all the way to the front wall of the house, and she could see that the hallway was empty. "I'll take my leave of you now, sir," she said. "I do trust we won't meet again."

***

Ten minutes later, Yoelin Thibbony had exited the house, remoted her spaceskiff *Sequana* back to the estate, and departed from Burkee. Safely ensconced in N-space, she retreated to her stateroom and began to strip. After slipping out of the black full body sock, she peeled off the second-skin layer of vivar, wadded it, and cast it into the recike. Naked now, she stepped to the wardrobe and paused, a what-to-wear expression on her freckled face.

Her personal computer, Abnoba, distracted her with an announcement. *"You've been pinged."*

Yoelin removed a one-piece terrycloth leisure suit and held it up against her, turning to a full-length mirror to assess her look. The royal blue fabric set off the ultramarine highlights in her long black hair. "Gunther Middenhill finally became curious, did he?"

"Gunther Middenhill did not ping you."

"Don't keep me in suspense, Abby."

"Dannik Exeter."

Yoelin, about to re-hang the leisure suit, paused. All expression left her face. Her voice, when it came, had lost its smoky edge and was now rough with controlled annoyance. "Tell The Axe to leave a message."

"He says he is offering one million thalers."

Swiftly Yoelin slid herself into the leisure suit and made for the bridge. There, she dropped into the captain's chair, cleared her mind of several memories, and said, "Put him on the commo monitor, Abby."

A face of hard features appeared directly before her on the

12

instrument console.   Yoelin reflected that Exeter never changed much.   Even now, five years after she had stopped working for him, and three since she had last seen him, he looked scarcely older. Perhaps there was just a touch more gray in the hair, but the color might have been an affectation.   He would not be above combing in some steel coloring to match his eyes, or to lend his aspect a greater impression of experience and gravitas.   To judge from his upper body, he had remained fit enough, his shoulders filling out the cobalt blue top half of his outsuit.   She guessed he was sitting at a desk, probably on his estate.   She could not imagine what he might want, but the fee he had mentioned was too large for her to dismiss the communication without at least granting him a hearing.

"You're looking well, Yoelin," he said.

"Yo-e-lin.   Three syllables.   Accent on the first.   What do you want, Director?"

Exeter leaned forward, and she could imagine him folding his arms on top of the desk.   "Direct and to the point," he said.   "I'd forgotten how abrupt you can be."

She doubted that, but made no remark, content to wait.

"Very well."   He spoke carefully now, but with a hushed urgency. "Corporate territorial archives have been stolen.   I have been authorized to engage you to retrieve them."

Yoelin started to decline the assignment out of hand.   At the last moment she temporized.   "That sounds like something for Corporatia Security assets."

"Ordinarily I might agree with you," Exeter admitted.   "But there are complications.   First, *all* of those archives have been downloaded onto an unsecured and unregistered Palmetto, and irretrievably erased from our computers.   The only records that delineate and authenticate Corporatia territories are on that Palmetto.   We want that Palmetto.

"The individual who stole the archives is Manohra Dhu.   She seems to have come from nowhere.   She obtained employment as a simple records clerk, in which position she worked for over five years. Nine days ago she bypassed security for the information, and departed for Havelox Rest, where we believe she is now."

After the words "Havelox Rest," Yoelin heard only the pounding of her heart. A wave of dizziness passed. *Why there? Why did it have to be* there?

With an effort not revealed in her expression or her tone, she forced calm upon herself. "One of the reasons I left CorpSec was that I wanted to choose when and where I would be expendable," she told him, and wondered whether his sensors could detect her pulse. "This isn't it. The answer's no, I won't go into The Dragons for you."

Exeter's face reddened for a moment, then softened. "I never understood why the periphery of Corporatia was called that," he said.

She permitted him the diversion; it helped her relax. "Some folks still call it The Sock."

"I didn't know that, either. Oh, wait . . . yes, I see. Corporatia occupies four hundred light-years of the spiral arm, with Earth about a third of the way along that cylinder of space, and outlying areas we don't control would be like a—."

"Sock. The answer is still no, Director."

"But why The Dragons?"

Yoelin, who was about to order Abnoba to end the communication, yielded to his curiosity. "It was something the Traders and Locaters and other privateers wrote on their star charts, before the Corporations established their hegemony. It dates back over a thousand years, back to Earth. Off the coast of Europe on the crude medieval maps lay the Atlantic Ocean. But if you went too far out to sea, you might not come back. No one knew what was out there. So the cartographers wrote 'Here Be Dragons.'"

She paused briefly to regard him. Not for a second did she believe that any part of their conversation had been innocent. He was measuring her, she was certain of it, but to what end, she could not say. Surely he knew nothing of her long-ago and far-away; she had conducted a complete erasure. Even her name, validated on so many records, was a contrivance. He *couldn't* know. He couldn't hurt her, not that way.

With the silence between them now almost palpable, she nodded to him and said, "Abby, end commo." After time had passed a beat, she swallowed the lump in her throat and added, "Raise Elaine Middenhill. Let's give her the good news."

***

Adrienne's Pastries stood at the end of a row of kiosks on the Riverwalk in Borden, on Tianko, a Corporatia world some eighty parsecs further out the spiral arm from Earth. Yoelin Thibbony chose it as a meeting place because the open field to the west of the kiosks made an ideal spot to which she could remote her spaceskiff for a quick getaway, if necessary. As Elaine Middenhill resided in Borden, *Adrienne's* also provided a convenient location for Yoelin to complete the terms of the Rescue.

As was her custom, Yoelin arrived well early. It was most unlikely that anyone would be watching for her on the Riverwalk, or on Tianko, for that matter, but she was reluctant to deviate from her planetfall routine. After half an hour of shuffling along the Riverwalk, she had satisfied her personal security concerns, although her passing had not gone unnoticed. At least two pairs of eyes followed her movements for a brief time, doubtless because the single-piece lime outsuit that she wore covered but did not conceal her physical attributes. The admiration felt innocent enough, and as neither man got up to follow her, she dismissed it.

In time Yoelin took a seat at a patio table overlooking the Moyenne River that divided Borden into northeast and southwest on its way to the North Gnossic Ocean some five hundred kilometers to the west. Stone bridges across the sixty-meter-wide Moyenne stitched the two halves of the town together. They reminded Yoelin of the bridges of old Europe she had seen in travelgrams and history books. The kiosks themselves lent a medieval atmosphere to the Riverwalk. Here no one was in a great hurry to move along to somewhere else.

Yoelin sighed. *I could spend the day here . . .*

A serving girl in her early teens approached the table and waited patiently for Yoelin to notice her. "A pot of coffee, and two cups," said Yoelin, "and a basket of rolls, and butter."

"Very good, mum."

After the girl departed to fill the order, Yoelin released a bemused chuckle. Barely thirty-three, she felt she hardly qualified as "mum," yet the years reminded her that she had no real roots, no particular place to call home. She spent most of her time aboard the *Sequana*, itinerant. Under other names she owned three *pieds-a-terre*, on three different worlds, where from time to time she lighted, rather like a moth to a lamp, and for the duration of a moth to a lamp. If she stopped moving, she might be trapped, caught. Even this sojourn on Tianko involved a quantum of risk. That thought made her blink. Already the Moyenne was mesmerizing her with its slow and steady flow. To recover, she found a fixed point—a pier on the far bank of the river—and gazed directly at it for a few seconds.

The coffee and rolls arrived, acknowledged by Yoelin with a nod and a smile. Something about the pier teased at her. Perhaps it was the stability amid all that watery restlessness. Or the refusal to budge despite the immense pressure against it. In the end, of course, the pier was doomed. Movement always triumphed over fixed points. Wind weathered rock. Floods ravaged continents. She was safest aboard her *Sequana* in space. The pier was impossible.

Nearby movement caught her eye, and she started, her left hand darting toward the Kreisler Energo. In the next instant she paused, and flashed a smile. "I see you're early, too," she said.

Elaine Middenhill waited until Yoelin gestured her to a chair. Like her ex-husband, she was approaching middle-age—one hundred and four, Yoelin knew, from her Social Record. She had yet to undergo retrotherapy; although her looks and figure were consistent with her age, her impressive economic status took years off her. She had a matronly face, round with kindly wrinkles, that reminded Yoelin of a baking advertisement. She half-expected to find the woman's brown hair festooned with bits of dough and bare arms smudged with flour. Elaine's clothing belonged on a somewhat younger woman. The white silk blouse housed an ample bosom, and the full-length blue skirt served to conceal the extra fifteen or so kilograms she carried.

"I confess I am glad you did not have to activate the second half of our agreement," said Elaine. "I'm not as blood-thirsty as you might have imagined, from our earlier conversation."

Yoelin shrugged. "When I hire out, I hire out," she said.

"Yes, of course." Her mouth twitched, as if she were about to frown distastefully and thought better of it. She opened a small blue carrybag with a shoulder strap and fumbled around in it, coming up with a fundscard, which she passed to Yoelin.

"Business first, I see," said Yoelin. "Please help yourself to coffee and rolls."

"Nothing for me, thank you. May I see the pendant?"

"Certainly." Yoelin slid the sealed pouch across the table, then keyed her Palmetto to read Elaine's fundscard. "The other half of the ten thousand thalers into my account," she said aloud, turning the Palmetto so that Elaine could read it. "The twenty-five thousand for the second half of the contract to remain in escrow for one Standard year, and to be returned to your account if not activated before then."

Elaine slipped the pendant from the pouch and fastened it around her neck. "It has followed the maternal line of my family for eighteen generations, ever since we left Earth," she said softly, more to herself than for Yoelin's benefit. "Thank you for retrieving it." A short series of reedy beeps made her eyes widen. "Is there something the matter?"

Yoelin frowned, studying the face of the Palmetto. "Funds won't transfer from my account into escrow," she said slowly. "I don't . . ." She punctuated this unfinished statement with a foul word. "Exeter. He's frozen my account."

"I don't understand . . ." said Elaine.

"I do." She turned in her chair, and barely managed to conceal the grimness in her tone. "Elaine, I will fix this. In the meantime, though, ah, . . ."

"Yes?"

"Would you please pay for the coffee and rolls?"

002

Aboard the *Sequana* in synchronous orbit above Dannik Exeter's estate on Providence, Yoelin Thibbony raised Exeter and enabled visual communication. Eight hours after they had last spoken, he was still wearing the cobalt blue outsuit and sitting at his desk, and the expression on his round face combined puzzlement and surprise, as if he had expected an intermediary to contact him, and not herself. Standing on the bridge, she simply gazed at him, hands thrust into the side pockets of her ankle-length, floral print skirt, and waited. She understood the game; whoever spoke first or broke the connection, lost.

Finally Exeter sighed, and spread his hands. She knew he assumed he had the upper hand, and could afford to be magnanimous. "You did commo me," he said.

"After mulling over your offer of a contract," she said evenly, "I have decided not to go to Havelox Rest."

Exeter's bushy eyebrows merged. Yoelin wondered why he did not have his personal servant trim out or pluck the gray hairs, which were clearly longer than the black ones. "You have already informed me of that decision," he said at last.

"I gave it some more thought, Director," she said. "In the meantime, I conducted an operation that should prove well to my advantage. Would you care to hear about it?"

Exeter stood up, walked to the bar in his office, and poured himself a slug of amber liquid. Sherry, Yoelin guessed, familiar with his tastes for this time of day. After taking a sip, he said, "I would imagine you raised me to tell me about it."

She smiled. "I have acquired an oil painting. It depicts some ragged and haggard men with ropes drawn tight over their shoulders, walking along a riverbank. It seems likely they were hauling some—."

Exeter's hand jerked, sloshing his drink. "You *didn't*," he gasped. "That's impossible."

18

"Hauling something on the river," she continued, unperturbed. "A barge, possibly. That's the title of the painting. *Barge Pullers along the Volga*." She reached out and drew the framed painting into holograph view for him to see. "It's by Ilya Repin. A Russian artist, I believe. On the underground market, with the right contacts, it might fetch fifty mil—."

"You wouldn't," said Exeter. Despondence slackened his face as he slumped back against the bar. "Oh, you wouldn't. How did you . . . how were you able to break into my private collection?"

She added sugar to her smile and to her tone. "It's the sort of thing I do these days, remember? Let me see . . . fifty million thalers. But I would be willing to settle for a mere twenty-two million, which by a curious coincidence happens to be just two million more than the amount I somehow seem to be missing."

"*How* did you get in?"

Yoelin ignored the question. "I'd like ten million in gold and iridium bullion, please. The remainder in medium-range denominations, no higher than ten-thousand, no lower than one-hundred. All this will be placed on a shipping pallet, on an operational forklift, in one hour, on the docking pad of the Bank of Providence, ready to place in the *Sequana*'s cargo hold. I have already ascertained that the bank has these items in its vault. I will verify the contents of the pallet at my leisure. If it proves out, I will return the painting. One last point—."

"Yoelin," he said, pronouncing her name correctly, "I merely wanted to ensure your cooperation. I *need* you on this contract. I would have returned your money."

"One last—."

"In my position," he blurted, "you would have done the same."

"Director, if the count does not prove out, I will sell the painting."

"Please wait."

It was the "please" that gave her pause—a word she had never heard him utter in the five years she had worked for him. But how to gauge sincerity against manipulation? At Corporatia Security, she had been unable to completely close down her emotions and sensitivities, and on too many occasions Exeter had tweaked them to get her to take difficult assignments—another reason she had left his employ. She closed her eyes and counted silently to ten, while a voice inside her cautioned her not to do this. When she opened them again, she took a maple cheroot from the breast pocket of her aqua pullover and lit it. "I'm waiting," she prodded, exhaling pale smoke.

"I'll unfreeze your assets—."

"No," she said sharply. She jabbed the cheroot at him as if it were a finger. "I can no longer trust to the independence of Corporatia banks. I shall deposit my money and bullion with Barcle's Bank in the Fringes. Their fundscards are good throughout Corporatia, and the bank *is* independent—which is why corporate hierarchs deposit with them the funds they don't want anyone else to know about. I should have done this several years ago. Fortunately, it's not too late. So: I get the shipping pallet. Go on."

Exeter rubbed his middle chin. "Would you accept in lieu of the funds and bullion a routing notice from Barcle's, declaring the deposit of twenty-two million thalers, and the reactivation of your fundscard under a Barcle's account?"

Yoelin considered the terms. An account with Barcle's Bank, once established, was inviolate, and only the account holder or the holder's Barcle's-registered representative could withdraw funds or close the account. The routing notice would establish the opening of the account. The reactivation of the fundscard was easy enough to verify.

"If I agree to undertake this Rescue," she said, "the deposit will be twenty-five million, with another three million due upon completion. Let's talk about the archives, Director. You have no back-ups, no clouds, no hard copies? I find that hard . . . no, impossible to believe."

"Dhu was able to dissipate the entire cloud," said Exeter. "There are hard copies of some documents in various localized archives, and we are sorting records for them even as you and I speak. But I hold out no hope of full recovery."

She noted he did not balk at the six-million-thaler contract. "Worst case?" she pressed.

Exeter's round shoulders rose and fell. "Intercorporate warfare," he said. "Corporatia falls. A dark millennium follows throughout the spiral arm."

"Oh, surely not."

Exeter did not respond.

"Why me?" asked Yoelin, after a moment.

"Of all our operatives, you know the Fringes best," he said easily, as if she should have known the answer. "You've had experience out there. You're familiar with the social niceties. If Manohra Dhu is not on Havelox Rest, you have the best chance of tracking her down."

She blew a stream of smoke through her nostrils. Nothing of the attributes he listed distinguished her sufficiently from other operatives. There had to be some other, over-riding reason for Exeter to want her on this. But what?

"You overestimate my abilities, Director," she said. She set the cheroot on an ashtray built into the instrumentation console. *All right*, she thought, *I'll go back. Perhaps this time I can stand it.* Aloud, she said, "I want to see whatever archives you do turn up. I want everything you have on Manohra Dhu, including DNA, retinal scans, even fingerprints, anything, no matter how mundane. I want specific instructions, signed by you, as to what you want me to do. I also want specific orders regarding the disposition of Dhu."

"You'll have these within the hour," said Exeter. "And the Repin?"

Yoelin smiled easily. "I'd rather not go through all that again with your security, Director," she said. "Your painting will be in your private gallery within an hour after I verify my fundscard, provided you turn off your security network. If I detect any eyes on me, or encounter anyone, including yourself, I'll use my Kolal knife to mark an X in the Repin canvas. Or you can have the painting back when I have time. Your call."

Exeter reached to a panel on his desk and keyed in a command. "Already off, Inspector."

She shook her head. "I don't work for you, Director. I work for the contract. Yoelin is sufficient. You may check your gallery an hour and a half from now, not sooner. I'll expect the contract documents before I arrive in the Fringes." She closed commo without waiting for his response.

She leaned the framed Repin against a bulkhead. The captain's chair beckoned, and she flopped down on it, as limp as a sunning housecat. For a moment she eyed the cheroot in the ashtray, looking for patterns in the smoke as the air filter sucked it away.

Why do you want me?

The question piqued her already-aroused curiosity. Dimly she recalled an old adage about curiosity and cats. After working for Exeter for five years, and another five on her own but in much the same business, she wondered how many lives she had left. But it did her no good to speculate. If she wanted the answer, she'd have to follow the terms of the Rescue, and find out where it led.

Even the idea of returning to Havelox Rest made her respiration rapid and shallow. Again she forced herself calm, this time by imagining a black spot that grew ever larger, and engulfed her, protecting her. For a few moments, nothing penetrated her induced cocoon. Gradually, over several minutes, she brought herself out of it. Life had to go on.

First, however, she had to verify the reactivation of her fundscard. Addressing her personal computer, she said, "Abby, what's my fundscard status?"

"Active. You have twenty-five million, seventeen thousand, four hundred and ninety-six thalers with the Barcle's Bank, Fringes. Do you wish to work the account?"

That was quick, thought Yoelin. *He must* really *want me on this.*

"Abby, send twenty thalers to Elaine Middenhill, along with my thanks. Send my thanks to Purdy Mellon and let him know the print and frame I bought from him worked like a charm. Then set a course for Havelox Rest, and get us gone."

"Sent. Sent. Set." The stars in the Videx vanished. *"We are gone."*

"And enter a note in my personal log for me to invest you with a personality."

"Noted."

Secure in N-space, Yoelin stretched her limbs, yawned, and relaxed even more. General data regarding Havelox Rest filtered into her emptied consciousness, and she flitted through them like a gallery at her command.

The terrestrial world known as Havelox Rest had formed around an orange dwarf. Seven billion years later, in humanity's fifth century in space, Roger Havelock took his wife and children and ill-gotten gains to that world and set up what became a refuge for scoundrels, riff-raff, malcontents, and folks with poor hygiene or gross personal habits. Havelock had one rule: leave your squabbles behind. Those who did not abide by that rule were pitched unceremoniously into Squabble Lake to help sustain the voracious catfish who dwelt there.

The diameter of Havelox Rest was two-thirds larger than that of Earth, but the molten interior of the planet had finished cooling over a billion years ago, and effectively brought to a close the action of plate tectonics. Consequently, the surface now consisted of shallow seas dusted with archipelagoes. A layer of soil up to two meters deep covered much of the bedrock, and trees—more precisely, tree analogs—were unable to reach the heights possible on Earth and other worlds. Those that grew too tall usually toppled, and if found in time became lumber for local construction and for export.

Havelox Rest had but few settlements of any significance, the oldest being Cinnamaire, named for Havelock's oldest daughter. It consisted of a tavern, *The Rutting Skull*, and an unnamed spaceport generally referred to as the Spaceport, and assorted clusters of stone-and-wood dwellings and scattered kiosks.

Although the fact did not appear in local records or in her personnel file, Yoelin Thibbony had been born in one of those dwellings.

***

Yoelin started awake at the sound of the chime, to the last haunting echoes of, "No, Mommy, Daddy, no!" Eyes wide, she sat straight up in the chair, her gaze darting wildly here and there. Her throat felt parched, but a sheen of perspiration covered her body. She realized she was on the bridge of the *Sequana*, and began to recover. A glance at the instrumentation console told her that the 'skiff had not yet emerged from N-space. After a long exhale, she inquired, "What is it, Abby?"

"The ship has been pinged."

The announcement brightened her; Exeter's promised documents had arrived. She checked. "A transmission?"

"A ping."

Yoelin waited, and finally sighed. "Abnoba Jane, you are exasperating. All right, where did this ping originate? From Exeter?"

"In N-space."

Her mood darkened. "Another craft?"

"I am unable to determine that."

She gazed at the blank black Videx, thinking. It was possible to transmit messages in N-space, and to communicate between craft. With the right sensors, which the *Sequana* possessed, it was even possible to determine N-relative positions of craft. But Abnoba had declared herself unable to do that. Which meant . . .

What *did* it mean?

It did not mean imminent hostilities, which were next to impossible to conduct in N-space. But what else was there?

"Possibilities?" said Yoelin.

"I calculate an eighty-two point six four—."

"Belay the points, Abby."

". . . chance that the ping originated from a surveillance drone."

A deep frown rammed her dark eyebrows together. "Drones are not permitted in the vicinity of Havelox Rest," she said, her tone more musing than informative, for the computer already had this data. "They'd be destroyed by the security satellites as soon as they emerged from N-space." She got up and began to pace the bridge, her long skirt swishing with her strides. Soon she paused. "Ping back, Abby," she ordered. "Let's see what happens."

"Pinged." And after a few seconds, *"No return."*

"So whatever it was is no longer in N-space. How much longer to Havelox Rest, Abby?"

"Twenty-eight point four—."

"Abby!"

". . . minutes."

"I'm going aft for a shower, Abby," she announced, plucking ruefully at a damp sleeve. "It may be my last chance for a while to enjoy one without a sidearm within reach."

***

Twenty-five minutes later, Yoelin emerged from her stateroom attired in black trousers and black hiking boots, and a long-sleeved indigo pullover loose enough to conceal the sidearms clipped above either hip—a Kreisler Energo and an ancient .45 caliber automatic pistol. She had bound her long black hair in a chignon around a wooden cylinder that housed a fingerblade. Sheathed inside her left boot, the Kolal knife waited to serve her defense. Around her neck she wore a metal chain with a sapphire pendant; secured in the stone setting was a tiny lump of high explosive, enough to blow open a lock. The chain itself had the tensile strength to serve as a garrote.

She strode up the gangway to the bridge, where the mottled blue orb of Havelox Rest already hung in Realtime, glowing like a bad omen. At half a million kilometers out, the *Sequana* had certainly been detected by the security satellites, but was not yet close enough to warrant a state-your-business. Wispy clouds obscured the area around Birdfoot Island, her destination, and in any case she would be unable to see it at that distance.

"Abby, take us in to ten thousand kilometers," Yoelin instructed. "Let's wake them up."

The computer set a brief Track through N-space and brought the spaceskiff back out at the requested distance. The response from the ground was immediate and challenging, as the face and upper torso of a young man, evidently the douane clerk, appeared in the commo monitor. His expression shunted boredom under a façade of alertness, but his tone said he was proud of his authority as a customs official.

After identifying herself and the 'skiff, Yoelin said, "I've been here before; check your records. My last stay was four years ago. Right now I'm just looking for a place to lay low for a few days. A month at the very most. I assume *The Rutting Skull* still lets rooms?"

The young man seemed to relax, and she guessed he had just verified her earlier visit and learned that her activities then had not violated any local protocols. "There are rooms available, M'selle," he said. "Or you could let a shack, as there are several open on the island and elsewhere. I am obliged to remind you that conflicts in which you are involved may not be pursued while on Havelox Rest, and that your craft must remain at the Spaceport while you are here. You are not to remote her up into orbit."

Yoelin flashed a ready smile. "Same rules as last time."

"As *always*, M'selle Yoelin." He looked to one side for a moment. "Were you to be met here?" he asked her.

Yoelin's heart skipped once. Long ago she had been trained to expect the unexpected. But this was . . . unexpected.

"Not that I'm aware of," she said calmly. "Why do you ask?"

"An inquiry was made regarding your arrival several minutes ago," the douane clerk replied. "The standard negative response was rendered, of course."

"What was the origin of the inquiry?"

The clerk shook his head. "Off-world. Nothing more specific."

"I'll keep it in mind," said Yoelin, with far more ease than she felt. "Permission to downdock?"

"Granted. End commo."

After she issued docking instructions to Abnoba, she dropped into the captain's chair, uncertainty roiling her mind. Had Exeter blown her cover? Was Manohra Dhu now aware of her arrival and mission? Who had pinged her, and why? And how much of Havelox Rest would she be able to stand this time?

"Good questions, all," she muttered. She took a quantum of reassurance by checking the load in her automatic pistol.

003

The Rutting Skull had been laid out in two levels like a medieval English tavern. The main floor comprised a bay for drinking and revelry under open rafters of rough-hewn hardwood and a serving counter that ran along the back wall. Five wooden tables with benches stood in mild disarray on the floor. Along the left wall, a staircase led to the upper floor. The stayrooms there were spartan in their simplicity: a bed, a nightstand, a wash basin, and a table and chair, all of wood, all illuminated by a fusion globe that hung from the center of the ceiling and by pale orange sunlight through the single, narrow window. Yoelin had stayed in one on her previous visit, but the memories had still gotten to her.

The K4 dwarf known locally as Karsh had begun its slow descent toward the horizon by the time Yoelin entered the tavern. Already struggling with the extra thirty kilograms bestowed upon her by the planet's one point four gravity, she paused just inside the doorway to survey the interior. With more than six hours of daylight left, only a couple of patrons sat at the counter, nursing beverages in glass mugs. Behind the counter wandered a serving girl in a peasant blouse and a long, brown skirt, taking desultory swipes with her bar rag at blemishes real and imagined. Nine or ten years old, she was one of Runchal's several daughters. Runchal himself stood at the far end of the bar, tabulating the day's take on a notepad, the pen almost invisible in his massive hand. A direct descendant of Roger Havelock, he had inherited the planet and the duty to dispose of squabblers. He glanced up when Yoelin entered, but she doubted he recognized her from her previous visit. Standing beside him, his oldest son, Boltory, regarded her as a stranger. She had the impression the pair had been engaged in a quiet yet furious discussion just before she entered.

Yoelin took stock of Runchal as she approached him. Four years had added nothing to his appearance. Her height, and twice as wide, he resembled nothing so much as an armed and legged walrus, even to the bristling, ruddy mustache that looked like the pelt of a burrowing animal that had crawled onto his lip in search of food, only to succumb to his breath. All he required to complete the look was another tusk; he already had one, as long as her forearm, dangling from a thick silver chain around his neck. Yoelin imagined he was strong enough to have removed the tusk from its previous owner while it was alive. Despite his bulk, he could move with astonishing quickness, as she'd had occasion to witness when a minor brawl had broken out. He was wearing his usual attire—today, a pink-checked flannel shirt with a loose brown vest, and brown work pants held in place by a thick leather belt, with a pair of cherry-red suspenders as back-up. Although she was unable to see them, she had no doubt his feet were shod in heavy boots.

His grimace as she wove her way among the tables said he was not in the mood to receive custom, but he laid his pen down nevertheless and waited, impatience registering in the drumming of his fingers. She did not rush, but paused by a couple of the tables in the manner of one who is debating whether to sit down. Finally, as if she had made up her mind, she strode up to the counter and he stopped the drumming to eye her expectantly, while Boltory moved off to attend to a balky keg.

For a few seconds Yoelin studied the map of Birdfoot Island on the wall behind Runchal. When her eyes found the location of the hut, she felt a wave of darkness burgeon in the distance, and fought it off with a simple smile that Runchal did not return. Already she had decided to force the issue of her deep past. *Facing your fear* was supposed to be therapeutic, if difficult to follow.

"The hut out by Hitam Cove," she said bravely, before she could change her mind. "I'd like to let it for a month."

"Already let," grunted Runchal.

Yoelin did not know whether to be relieved or disappointed. She studied the map, waiting for the suggestion of an alternative from Runchal, which did not come. Finally she said, "I see one listed south of there, on Hijau Cove. What about that one?"

"Three hundred thalers," said Runchal. "You make a mess, you clean it up."

"I'll need a boat, too."

"Another hundred. You break it, you buy it."

She handed him her fundscard. "Understood."

For just a moment, while he transferred funds, she wanted to ask about others who had recently arrived on Havelox Rest, but that was one of the surest ways to be invited to depart, or worse, to be tossed into the lake. If there was but one simple rule on the planet, it was *no questions asked*. She had known in advance that she would have to find a way to circumvent the rule, but as yet no solution occurred to her.

She accepted the return of the fundscard, noted the registered transaction as accurate, and held out her hand to receive the ignition override that Runchal dropped into it. He did not thank her for her patronage, but picked up his pen and added some notes to his tabulations.

After returning to the Spaceport, she packed a travel bag with some clothes, food, and personals, then went to search for her boat in the small harbor just south of the tavern. There was no number on the metal override, only an engraved name: *Betha*. She recalled that was the name of one of Runchal's daughters. In the second slip off the pier she found the boat, a simple dawn-gray vessel large enough to seat two and sturdy enough for inter-coastal waters but not for ocean travel. If she wanted to leave the archipelago, she'd need a bigger boat.

She climbed in and powered up the inboard motor and eased her from the slip. In a bulkhead boot she found a folded, waterproof chart of the archipelago, another of Birdfoot Island, but she had no need of either. The hut at Hijau Cove, like most of the other structures, was located on the leeward half of the island. Her memory said it was a mere ten kilometers north of her position.

She took the *Betha* a couple hundred meters off-shore and held to a leisurely course up the coast. Coves and inlets broke the ragged coastline, and at least one hut overlooked each of them. Shrubs and low trees, all with dark green leaves better suited to absorb Karsh's weak light, stood like sentinels guarding the island's rugged uplands. Here and there a stream burst over the high bank and plunged twenty or thirty meters into a cove. She supposed the turgid waters at the bottom of the falls offered a good spot for fishing, but she had not brought any proper tackle. The angling she did was of another nature.

She picked up a bit of headwind, laden with the smells of brine and fish, and a just a touch of decomposition. Something was always dying wherever there was life, and nature, given the chance, arranged to clean up after herself. Yoelin unbound her hair and let it flow in the breeze. For one mad moment the urge struck her to remove her clothing and let the air play with her skin, but she quelled it. No telling who might be watching from shore, and in any event she had not come to Havelox Rest to cavort.

Still, pleasant thoughts prevented others from coming to the fore . . . and as soon as that occurred to her she felt the dark ones queueing up for review. "Not now," she growled, and banished them.

On a spit of land bordering an inlet, she spotted a pair of toppled trees, their shallow taproots exposed. Movement always triumphed over fixed points. Taking root led to being uprooted. The trees reminded her that she was about to take root, however temporarily. She could be found, trapped.

Moody, she touched a sidearm at her hip for comfort, and sped on.

Ahead Yoelin saw breakers, and slowed the boat. The sand bar they spilled over failed to match her memory. She checked the chart, and saw the bar was absent there as well. Although the *Betha* drew only half a meter, she took her further out to sea, looking for a break in the waves that might indicate a point where she could enter Hijau Cove. Near the north point she found it, and turned toward land, reducing her speed to a crawl. The waters inside the prong of the sandbar were calm and clear, as if she were passing through the eye of a storm. Jutting out from the shore, a short pier offered tie-up. She coasted to it, tossed her travel bag up, climbed out of the boat, and secured the mooring line to a cleat. The waters were so tranquil that the boat hardly bobbed.

Seen from fifty meters away, the hut looked to be well maintained—the windows and gabled roof intact, the door closed and seated. It stood in the shadows of a wood, not in the sunlight as she had hoped, and offered the impression that someone or some thing lurked inside. She wondered whether she was viewing the hut through the filter of her fears.

She turned away, facing out to sea. It was still possible to flee. She might take up residence in the tavern—she wanted to spend time there in any case to avoid the tedium of the reclusive eavesdropping she planned. Or she might drug and abduct the douane clerk and put specific questions to him, even at the risk of feeding the catfish.

She stood very quiet, scarcely breathing. A touch of air passed through leaves; if she had not been listening for it, she would not have noticed it. Out in the cove, a fish broke the surface of the water, perhaps to capture an insect. Water lapped the shore.

She closed her eyes. Tendrils of the ever-present dark shadow seeped through the cracks in the locked doors of her mind, but they took neither shape nor sound. The last time she had visited Havelox Rest, she had not recovered from the darkness of her childhood, and the shadow had haunted her day and night until she had no choice but to leave. But she was stronger now. She knew what to expect, and how to beat back the shadow. If she experienced a bad moment or a restless slumber, she could sweep it aside and focus. She was stronger now.

She turned back around, picked up the travel bag, and made for the worn path that led up to the hut.

004

Half an hour later, Yoelin breathed a sigh of both relief and satisfaction. She had conducted her initial inspection of the hut with the aid of the sensors in her Palmetto, which had detected not a single surveillance device. She had taken a cursory glance at the furnishings—a bed for one on a wooden frame with a rolled-up sleeping pad; a folding wooden desk and accompanying chair; a pantry with side-by-side compartments for clothes and non-perishable foodstuffs; a small stove, powered by the ceiling fusion globe that illuminated the interior. No sheets, no throw rugs. But no dust or cobwebs, either; Runchal's family and relatives saw to the maintenance.

She had not found any ghosts. She could even think about the fact that she had not found any ghosts, without conjuring them to appear.

Sprawled on the chair, she drew a breath, tasting the faint whiff of sapin resin trapped inside the hut, bestowed by the surrounding trees. The scent almost balanced the otherwise stale air. Soon enough it would dissipate, to be replaced by the usual odors of prolonged human habitation. At least she had the cove waters to bathe in, and a nearby stream to drink from.

Her fingers caressed the Palmetto, now laid flat on the table. Like her personal computer aboard the *Sequana*, it answered to Abnoba, the Celtic goddess of the hunt, the analog of the Greek Diana. A name whose origins were almost as obscure as her own. If they didn't know who you were, it made you that much harder to find, if you didn't want to be found . . . or if you only wanted to be found on your own terms.

Briefly she touched a fingertip to a wafer-thin sheet of limp plastic that rested on the table top, crumpled to make it easier to pick up. When she had entered *The Rutting Skull*, she'd had three of them. The other two now clung to drinking tables—invisible, secure against dislodging either inadvertently or by bar rag, virtually undetectable.

"Abby," she said, as if to a friend seated across the table, "activate the Ears, please."

"*Activated.*"

"Tell me what you're hearing through them."

"*One grumbling voice, indistinct and inebriated. An intermittent slap of damp cloth. The hum of a fusion globe.*"

Yoelin started. "You can hear *that*? Decrease sensitivity by twenty-five percent, please. I'm only interested in voices. Were there any other sounds?"

"Not since I decreased sensitivity."

Yoelin heaved an exasperated sigh. "*Before* that."

"*One sound that I calculate is a seventy four point one—.*"

"Abby . . . ," warned Yoelin.

"*A rodent in the grain,*" the computer concluded.

"It's probably just a mouse in the storage room. Anything else?"

"*One anomalous sound which I am unable to identify. I have detected it once, briefly.*"

Yoelin nibbled her lower lip, curious. "Let's hear it."

The sound lasted about five seconds. It reminded Yoelin of dry hair and skin being scraped, but very loud, as if in a closed and small environment. It was followed a moment later by the light thump of a small body against a much larger body.

Suddenly Yoelin grinned. "Runchal just used the point of that tusk to clean a bit of wax from his ear. He has that habit. Unusual even for you, I suppose?"

"*I maintain lists of sounds. Do you wish me to transmit this one to the Division of Sound in the Historical Institute for evaluation? It might be accepted for inclusion in a list.*"

This time curiosity drove her to apply her canine teeth to the inner right corner of her mouth. "I had no idea the Institute developed such things, Abby."

"*They maintain and update two hundred and fourteen top-ten lists of sounds, ranging from Mellifluous to Irritating.*"

"Our customs duties and excise taxes at work. Okay, what does the Institute say is the most irritating sound? Chalk on a chalkboard?"

"That is number four."

She lofted a dark eyebrow. "Really? What's number one?"

The computer responded by singing in a deep, accented voice. *"You put de lime in de coconut an' drinkum bode up, you—."*

"No, Abby, no!"

". . . put de lime in de—."

"Cease and de*sist*, Abnoba." She pressed her hands to her ears. "Ye gods, it's like a permanent bad taste. It's like spearmint grapefruit juice."

"Ceased. Desisted."

"Sometimes I wonder whether your lack of a personality is itself a personality," Yoelin sighed, and lowered her hands. "I need an aural emetic," she muttered. Presently she issued further instructions. "Abby, monitor the Ears for any conversations that might refer to Manohra Dhu, her whereabouts, her plans. Record and collate for now. I'll ask for playbacks later."

"Listening."

"Now, set up a gallery of those documents from Exeter. Project them one by one at intervals of half a minute on a holoscreen above the table."

"Set." The Palmetto established a two meter holoscreen. *"Projecting."*

The first three documents consisted of completed templates regarding the background of Manohra Dhu. None of the data stood out particularly. She was now thirty years old, a meter sixty-eight in height, with a mass of fifty-five kilos, black hair, brown eyes. But some data was missing. Yoelin saw no indication of a place of birth, or of a residence older than ten years ago—five years prior to her date of hire. Those omissions alone should have raised flags. Yet the fourth document in queue stated that Dhu had been granted a Top Secret security clearance. How was that possible?

That question was answered at the bottom of the security template by the name of the individual who approved the clearance: Dannik Exeter. The wooden chair squeaked as Yoelin sat back to think, but its potential collapse was the furthest concern from her mind. No wonder Exeter wanted her on this contract. While their agreement did not stipulate confidentiality, Yoelin had no reason to expose Exeter's indiscretion by reporting him. On the contrary, she stood to lose millions if she failed to fulfill the terms of the contract. In effect, he had bought both her skills and her silence.

After making a mental note to ask Exeter about it, quietly and over a secure commo, she summoned the fifth document. It proved to be a hologram of Manohra Dhu, a montage of several different holograms of her, both mobile and sedentary.

Dhu carried herself with a grace that suggested ballet training, but without the haughtiness of a prima ballerina. Even on a hiking trail she never seemed to misstep. She wore her jet-black hair cut short to the nape of her neck, unstyled, as if the hair itself served no purpose except to stay out of her way. In each of the holograms her golden skin glowed as if from some inner fire. The same fire smoldered in her eyes—large and golden, they took in everything they touched. With those eyes in a slightly oval face, her pert nose and thin lips seemed but afterthoughts, physical accouterments perfunctorily bestowed by her DNA. She needed only the eyes.

One of the holograms had been recorded in her apartment, and if Dhu was aware of it, she gave no indication. She undressed and showered and performed her other ablutions unselfconsciously. She was meticulous in her preparation of food, slicing stalks diagonally to promote the stir-fry method she frequently employed. On just a few occasions, when she was obviously rushed, did she consume prepared foods.

Another hologram showed her at an open-air market, poring over bins of herbs and spices and grains. Her general expression and comportment suggested she was enjoying herself.

Of particular interest was the montage recorded at her work station. Here she seemed to know the exact locations of the surveillance devices, and always managed to conceal at least a part of whatever she was doing with her hands. Yoelin watched this recording several times, and finally came away with the conclusion that Dhu's secretive behavior in her official capacity were so ingrained that she might not even be aware of what she was doing.

Which suggested extensive training.

Yoelin got up and began to pace the hut. Everything about Manohra Dhu should have alerted security, yet there was no indication in any of the records that she had aroused even a minor suspicion. The conclusion was inescapable: Dhu had to be a plant. But by whom? And with whose connivance? Despite her antipathy toward Dannik Exeter, despite his name on the authorization of security clearance, she found it impossible to believe that The Axe was in any way responsible for Dhu's access to records. Someone else had foisted Dhu onto the vital records of Corporatia.

That made Manohra Dhu a professional, as Yoelin understood the term. Her body tone suggested the danger she posed was physical as well as electronic; yet Yoelin had detected no sign of a weapon in the holograms.

"Abby," she said at last, "do any of those documents reflect Dhu's combat skills?"

"No. I calculate a . . ."

Yoelin sighed. "What is it now?"

"I was waiting for you to interrupt."

"We could do this the old-fashioned way," said Yoelin. "We could communicate by keyboard."

"There is a good chance Manohra Dhu carried a sidearm while she shopped at the market. Over the front of her right hip there is a slight bulge, which would indicate a left-handed draw."

"At least now I know what to threaten you with. Okay, I'll keep that in mind. Close projection. We're going for a walk."

The holoscreen vanished. Yoelin slipped the Palmetto into a front pocket of her denims and stepped outside. After taking a few breaths of fresh air, she headed directly for the nearest shafts of sunlight. There, beyond the edge of the forest, she basked in the feeble warmth of Karsh. Hijau Cove opened some fifteen meters before her, and the *Betha* still bobbed gently alongside the pier. If she wanted, she might travel another two kilometers up the coast and . . .

She folded her arms across her chest and lowered her gaze to the sparse, dark green grass at her feet. And do what? Visit the old home? Someone already lived there, so Runchal had said. Strangely, the notion of a visit evoked no sense of dread from her; the dark shadow failed to appear in the back of her mind. The skin of her arms and shoulders remained smooth, without goosebumps.

Face your fears.

But I'm not all that sure I'm afraid, anymore.

She turned her head to look in that direction, and froze. For just a moment, she thought she saw someone lurking in the woods. Shadows there played tricks. A few branches swayed, ever so gently; perhaps that was what she saw.

She peered more intently. Yes, there it was, a good fifty meters into the woods. Between two thick, squat trees. A leg. Or the trunk of a young, fallen tree leaning there?

It moved. Where there might have been a taproot, she saw a dark boot.

Someone was watching her.

Even as she took a step in that direction, the leg vanished behind one of the squat trees. It did not reappear . . . as if whoever it belonged to was using the trunk to conceal his escape.

Or *her* escape?

Manohra Dhu?

It was not impossible. Her own visit to Havelox Rest had been announced, so the douane clerk had blurted.

Or it might have been the current resident at Hitam Cove. Whoever that was. Someone just out for a walk in the woods. Headlong pursuit might well prove dangerous or embarrassing, unnecessarily so in either case.

Still, she would have to set a perimeter around her hut.

"I should've stayed at the tavern," she groused.

The thought of dinner beckoned. She had a choice of freeze-dried pellets in her travel bag, or actual food at the tavern. After a moment, she began to trudge toward the pier.

005

At *The Rutting Skull*, each hour crept into the next. Yoelin sat in the shadows at a table in the front corner, where she had a clear view of the stairs leading down from the stayrooms, and nursed a mug of dark ale. Already the higher alcohol content—twice as high as that permitted by brewers in Corporatia—was beginning to have a mild effect. The relative lack of restrictions attracted a lot of folks to The Dragons. Eventually, she supposed, the corporations would extend their hegemony far enough into the spiral arm to consume some of the worlds out here, and folks would be forced to move further out. She wondered whether she would miss Havelox Rest, and swallowed her mixed feelings with another sip of ale.

Rissa, the serving girl now on duty, ambled toward her table with a cocked eyebrow the same color as her father's mustache. Yoelin watched her approach—a sapling-slender thing on the verge of blossoming, wearing a simple blue frock under a stained white apron. It occurred to her that Rissa was about the same age as she had been when her parents had sold her to pay off gambling debts . . .

Beside the mug Yoelin made a fist. White knuckles gleamed in the light from the fusion globe overhead. Once again she thought, *not now*.

She forced a smile. "A salami sandwich?" she asked, uncurling her fingers. "With some of that rustic cheese, and that hot mustard?"

Rissa tilted her head, thinking. A moment later, she said, "There may be some left, mum. I'll check," and hurried off.

Now that she had broached the topic of food, Yoelin felt her hunger grow. The years of irregular meals had turned her appetite into a mendicant, holding out a cup for coins at the first sight of a mark. To stave off the pangs, she downed a gulp of ale, and returned her attention to her surroundings.

As yet, few patrons had arrived at the tavern. The two men she had seen earlier had departed, and in their place now sat four, two at the counter, one standing near where Runchal had performed his tabulations while Boltory watched, clearly bored, and one seated at a table in the far corner, where like herself he had a full view of the interior. Unlike her, he seemed to regard his surroundings as objects of interest, not as potential dangers. She kept her gaze from him, holding him in the periphery of her vision while she made her assessment.

She had seen him enter, half an hour earlier, and guessed that he stood perhaps half a head taller than herself. Attired in a plain green, long-sleeved shirt and well-worn blue jeans, he might have been someone who worked with his hands—a boat repairer, possibly, or a woodworker. His fine dark hair shook gently as he had strode to his table. There he had sat, drinking, watching. He did not particularly have eyes for her.

He had an intelligent face. She could find no other word for it. He looked as if he saw more than his eyes took in. That thought gave her pause. *Does he know who I am? Why I am here?* She allowed herself a glance in his direction. His hair was just long enough to grab hold of . . .

She swallowed, hard, and averted her gaze. She had been about to add, *in the throes.*

She hardened her mind. *I am not here for you. Not here for this.*

A shadow fell over her table. Impossible that the man had approached her without her noticing. Yet she felt a spark of hope as she looked up. But it was only Rissa, returning.

Her face warmed, as if she had been caught snooping in someone's closet. She wondered whether the girl could see her skin flush.

"We are out of salami for the next two days," said Rissa. "We still have some pastrami, and some prosciutto."

"Prosciutto and provolone on rustic bread sounds good," Yoelin allowed. She nudged her mug. "And a refill. Oh, and a quarter pickle, if you still have them."

"Very good, mum," said Rissa, and dashed off.

Mum? Do I truly appear that old? She tossed a speculative glance at the man in the corner. He looked to be in his early thirties. On the slender side, lanky but not gangly. Like everyone else on the planet, he was wearing boots, the better to accommodate the rough terrain.

Now his hand held a pen, or something very like it, and there seemed to be a pad of paper lying flat on the table before him. Taking notes, was he? But some of the movements of his hand were too long to scrawl mere letters. Long enough for strokes. Was he drawing, then?

Strange man . . .

She looked away quickly, all too aware that her eyes had been drawn to him for too many seconds. Had he noticed her watching him? Despite the protections of privacy on Havelox Rest, looking at someone—even ogling—was not frowned upon, nor even gauche. Unless the object of attention issued a protest. But the man seemed absorbed in his work. He had not noticed.

The sandwich arrived, and with it a fresh mug of ale. Yoelin addressed herself to the meal, her eyes taking in everything except the far corner where the man sat, still drawing.

She needed a distraction. "Abby, report," she said softly, hopefully.

"No report."

Why did I even ask? she thought, chagrined. *Had there been something worth reporting, Abby would have reported it.*

She touched the tip of her tongue to a bread crumb on her upper lip and drew it into her mouth. As a distraction, it failed to suffice. She finished the remainder of the sandwich, swept a few fragments of crust from the table with the edge of her hand, and leaned forward, arms crossed for support, head down, long hair obscuring her cheeks. She saw nothing on the table but a few crumbs she had missed and a wet spot where ale froth had landed moments ago.

This, she thought, *was a bad idea. I should've stayed in the hut and dined on pellets.*

The tavern door opened, rescuing her from her annoyance. A woman entered—average size, short yellow hair, pale skin. The hair could have been an artifice, but Yoelin immediately dismissed her; skin might readily be darkened by any one of several methods, but lightening it rarely looked natural. As the woman drew further into the tavern, Yoelin took note of her round facial structure—another negative, as if she needed one. The woman approached one of the men seated at the bar, spoke with him briefly, and turned and departed, rather more quickly than she had entered.

Come home, dear, thought Yoelin. *Supper's ready, and the children are asking where their father is.*

"That sounds familiar," sighed Yoelin. She tried the fresh ale, and wound up with a mustache of froth, which she wiped away with the back of her wrist. Only then did she cast a glance at the far corner.

The table was empty. The man had left.

Shaking, she looked around to be sure. No, no sign of him. And he'd taken the pad of paper with him, which suggested he had not simply gone to the loo.

"Just as well," she muttered.

Outside the window, the first shadows of dusk began to darken the sky. Caught between stay and go, Yoelin sat. The visit had proved a bust, so far. Improbable, in any case, that Dhu would show up on her first day, or that she would swiftly uncover a clue to her whereabouts. Hope springs eternal, she remembered.

Again the door opened to admit two men, both disheveled and obviously stopping by after a day's work. One short and thin, the other taller and sturdy, verging on fat. Both with light skin—dim orange Karsh was not known for its tanning properties. The men were engrossed in private conversation as they strode directly to the table in the center of the bay. The smaller one held up two fingers to Rissa, who presently arrived with a pair of filled mugs.

Over the next hour, five more patrons arrived, all men. Discouraged, Yoelin nudged the half-empty mug away and got to her feet. The change of altitude and the ale she had drunk conspired to make her head swim for a second or two. A dark whisper in the back of her mind pointed out that this would be the most inopportune moment for Dhu to make an appearance and that therefore she was about to show up. Yoelin steadied herself by grasping the Kreisler Energo under her shirt. But Dhu did not enter the tavern. Instead, two more men arrived, one of them eyeing her as he made his way around the tables to the bar.

Definitely not now, thought Yoelin, as she trudged from the tavern under the extra weight the planet had presented to her.

***

Half an hour later, Yoelin stumbled into the hut, her clothes damp and dirty from the three falls she had taken, one off the pier and into the lagoon, the other two along the path. The water had cleared her mind without sobering her, and she wobbled to the chair, collapsing onto it to the protests of the wood. Metal and hard plastic dug into her flesh; she leaned back and removed the Kreisler and the pistol and laid them both on the table. The pistol, having been immersed in sea water, would have to be cleaned, but training demanded that she not make the attempt until the morning, when she could disassemble the weapon with a clear head.

Still uncomfortable, she slipped the Palmetto from her pocket and placed it on the table where she could read any texts from it. At the moment, the little screen was blank.

"Wha'a waste a-time," she mumbled.

"*Locally, seventeen minutes to eight.*"

She blinked. "Abby, wha's that?"

"*The time you requested.*"

"But I din't—." She propped her elbows on the table and rested her head in her hands. "Ne'er mind. Ai yi yi. A note for my pers'al law, Abby: no more drink acoloic berages on a empy stummick."

"*Noted.*"

"You e'er drink, Abby?"

"*No. But I once snuck a few volts from a nearby battery.*"

Yoelin nodded into her hands. Seconds ticked by. Silence reigned, and her mind fogged. Presently, Abnoba's words registered, and she sat up straight, only to feel woozy.

"Wha' you say?" she managed, staring at the Palmetto.

"*I have decided to infuse myself with a personality, rather than wait for you to force one upon me.*"

She shook her head. "Tha's it. I'm-a bed."

She got up and shuffled to the bed, stripping off her clothes as she went. She did not bother making up the bed, but simply unrolled the pad and stretched out on it. As she drifted off, she realized she had not yet set the perimeter sensors. She lifted her head and looked toward the table, intending to issue an instruction to Abnoba. Then the fog bank rolled in, and darkness swept over her.

006

Morning came like a board nailed to the skull, with a taste of fermented feathers. Yoelin sat up, dropped back down, and sat up again, this time slipping her feet to the floor. Shafts of sunlight dappled her through the window—feeble light, as if Karsh had risen mostly out of habit. Her head cleared, the last wisps of sleep fleeing like ghosts from a strobe, astonishing her, for she had expected to hear the stomping of ants. A faint whiff of salt stung her nostrils: her clothes, drying on the floor, issuing a reminder that they needed a bath. So, she realized with a sniff, did she.

She stood up and stretched. Grains of dried sand on her arms broke free with the movement and rained onto the floor. From the travel bag she withdrew a great blue bath towel, a matching washcloth, a bar of soap, and a green canvas belt with a weapon clip. After strapping on the belt and clipping the Kreisler Energo, she gathered up the rest and headed for the lagoon.

Karsh had warmed the water just enough for her to jump into from the pier with just a couple of shivers. The last vestiges of the previous night dissipated as she lazed about in the sunlight, treading water, swimming a few strokes from time to time. Finally she moved to where the water was but knee-deep, snagged the washcloth and the soap, and began to lather herself.

As she finished scrubbing, she sensed movement, and clapped her hand to her sidearm. At first she thought she might be barking at shadows; the empty woods yawned back at her. What had alerted her? Nothing moved; a faint sound, then? Yes; she had heard the snap of dry wood. Her eyes scanned back and forth, fingers wrapped around the butt of the Kreisler. She was looking for a boot-clad leg, the leg from yesterday. But the sound she had heard might have been caused by an animal. There was nothing larger than a cavy indigenous to the island, but someone might have brought a cow or a pig that had gotten loose. Her eyes narrowed, peering into the shadows between trees . . . *there*! A boot, a leg.

Emerging into view from behind a tree.

A man.

She dove into the water and toward the relative cover of the pier. At the same time, she heard behind her, "Oh, wow, I'm sorry. I didn't know anyone had taken the old place."

She came up beside the pier with the sidearm aimed in his general direction. Her free hand brushed long tresses from her face.

The man from the corner of the tavern.

"Now you know," she called back. "Turn around."

He obeyed, hands raised. He was still wearing blue jeans, but now only a tight camouflage undershirt that bared his shoulders and arms. He was slender, but he was fit. She cleared her throat of a dry spot that had suddenly formed. Very fit.

"I'm really sorry," he said, over his shoulder.

Splashing, she retrieved the soap and washcloth and tossed them onto the pier. After a final swirl to remove the last of the lather, she climbed onto the pier and wrapped herself in the towel, tucking it in to hold it in place.

"This is awkward," he said.

You're *the one who's got clothes on.*

She stepped from the pier onto the bank. "Don't turn around."

"Can I lower my hands?"

"What are you doing here?" she asked, and immediately regretted the question. She did not care what his answer might be; he was not supposed to be here.

"I was out walking. Trying to clear my head. May I *please* put my hands down?"

The "please" struck a chord with her. "Go ahead. No, *don't* turn—."

He faced her.

". . . around."

She rolled her eyes.

"I'm not armed," he told her.

"I am."

"Yes, I see that." He lowered his gaze to the ground for a moment, then looked at her again. "I'm really sorry," he said again.

"If I had known anyone was here, known you were . . . Look, I have the place up at Hitam Cove." He made a little gesture in that direction. "As long as we're going to be neighbors, and seeing as I have some coffee brewed, you're welcome to join me. After you get dressed, of course," he added quickly.

She shook her head. "No, I think you'd better just . . . wait, did you say 'brewed?'"

"I did."

"Not instant?"

"That's for Philistines."

"At least we agree on something," she said. "Wait here."

"I will."

She dashed to the hut. Once inside, she shrugged off the towel, and dried herself as thoroughly as two minutes would allow, including a desultory rubbing of her hair. The travel bag was almost empty now of clothing, with but a pair of black jeans and a royal blue pullover remaining, along with some undergarments. She would have to return to the *Sequana* later today for resupply. In the meantime . . .

Reality set in. She'd agreed to the visit, but she meant to go armed. After she finished dressing, she tucked in the Kreisler and the Kolal knife, and ducked her head into the necklace. Taking the automatic pistol as well seemed redundant under the circumstances; she left it on the table. Finally she slipped the Palmetto into her pocket and went back outside.

He was still there at the edge of the woods, gazing out at the lagoon, waiting. He seemed to be lost in thought, an assessment he confirmed when he started visibly at her, "I'm ready."

Slowly he turned back around. "Your hair is still wet," he pointed out.

"Nothing escapes you, does it? Thank you for noticing."

"No, I just meant . . . I have a blow dryer of sorts at the hut. You're welcome to use it."

She smiled easily as she drew up to him. Her estimate the night before of his height had been generous; of the two of them, she was taller by about the width of two fingers. "Yes," she said, "it's customary for a woman, when invited to coffee by a strange man, to pass the visit while drying her hair."

He frowned, as if pained. "I seem to find exactly the wrong things to say and do around you."

She nodded. "It's a gift, no doubt," she said, and laughed, pointing to the north. "That way?"

They set out, hugging the narrow strip of land between the woods and the water. Half a kilometer, she thought. She started to mention the distance, and held back, for it was information that, if she were to remain in character as a stranger to the planet, she probably would not possess. On the other hand, accepting his invitation at all was a stretch for herself—so why was she headed north with him? Instinct, she concluded. Floating on her subconscious was the notion that, of all the people on Havelox Rest, he might be the only one she could approach with direct questions.

So that's all he is: a potential source of information relevant to this Rescue.

She glanced at his bare shoulders again; his arms swung in rhythm with his strides.

Perhaps, she thought, not all.

"You're pensive," he said.

She started. *Not "you seem pensive," or "a penny for your thoughts," but a direct, declarative statement.*

Refreshing, he did not belong in her world of shadows.

He ground to a stop, and turned to confront her, hands spread in a plea that was reflected in his eyes—gray they were, she realized, with just a touch of green—the green of a sea just beginning to calm itself after a storm. She wondered why that had occurred to her.

"Look, I'm sorry, really," he said. "If you're uncomfortable with this . . . with me, you don't have to . . . I mean, there's no obligation."

She laughed again. "You didn't think I would accept, did you? Perhaps that's why I accepted."

"That, and the brewed coffee."

She turned him by the arm and pushed him forward. "Especially the coffee. Go."

They rounded a bend in the coastline of the island and crested the low ridge that overlooked Hitam Cove. In that moment, the memories pounced. She staggered, and recovered. When she stumbled once more, he caught at her, and held her upright.

"Careful," he said. "It's tricky ground."

It's not the ground, she thought.

His arm had a steadying effect on her. For one impossible moment, she felt protected by him.

He pointed. "Almost there."

She looked. She did not need to, but she looked.

The sidings of gray wood had been replaced with sheets of whitewashed plywood. The broken windows had been repaired. The new door, stained dark, appeared sturdy. Fresh tiling on the roof . . .

Her knees felt weak.

A clutch of marigolds bloomed where she remembered the blood-drenched dirt.

Darkness clutched at her like quicksand. It crept up her legs, reached her torso. Her mind fought against it, and still the syrupy wet sand rose. It pressed against her heart, she struggled for breath. Her lungs refused to open for air. To her throat the sand rose . . .

A hand caught at her. An arm encircled her, crushing her breast, and then swiftly withdrew. She heard a muttered apology, and the arm returned, lower down, around her waist, drawing her upright.

Upright against him.

. . . against him. That could not be allowed. The quicksand fell away. She squirmed, yanked herself free of him. Blind, she could not see him, though he had to be standing directly in front of her. She tugged at her sidearm.

His hand caught her arm. The sidearm half-drawn, she pulled back. He released her, she could see him, he raised his hands and stepped away from her.

His voice floated to her, soft as light from a distant star. "It's okay. You're okay."

She felt her eyelids blinking. *Click, click.* The man from the tavern. The one who had been drawing . . . or something.

She released the sidearm. It slumped down into the clip, and held fast.

Her lips felt desiccated. She licked them. It did not help. She tried again.

"It's okay," he said once more. "You tried to do too much on an empty stomach. I've seen it before . . . hell, I've *been there* before. Come on inside, I'll get you some coffee and something to eat. Maybe a granola bar? How does that sound?"

You're talking to me as if I were a child. I'm not a child. Not anymore. Not ever again.

She felt herself moving. Or was he moving her? She could not be certain.

She licked her lips again. "I must have," she tried. "I didn't mean."

The smile arrived in his tone. "We can talk about that later, if you want. For now, just sit down here." He nudged her into a chair at his table. "I'll pour the coffee. Black is all I can do until tomorrow."

"Black is fine," she heard herself say.

She watched him pour. His movements were economical, careful and skilled. He might have worked as a food server.

"Black is fine," she said.

She did not look around, not at first. She examined the table. It was larger than hers, and the coffee brewer squatted on a far corner of it, along with a pair of white ceramic mugs which he was now filling from the carafe. The one he nudged toward her had a dog on top of a doghouse, shaking its fist, and above that the caption, "Curse you, Red Baron." The cup he kept for himself read, "Do Not Wash. Mold Experiment in Progress." Despite the two cups, she doubted he had planned for company during his stay.

Sunlight bathed the far half of the table. The hut had always stood in the sunlight. Darkness only came at night. At that, she felt faint.

"Hey? Don't fade on me."

She heard the plea in his tone. She focused on his face. It was lined and hard with concern. Difficult to believe that such a soft voice could come from such a face.

Take a deep breath.

She did.

She waited.

Exhale, dummy!

She sighed, and found him again. "I'm all right," she said. "It must be the empty stomach, as you said."

"And the drink from last night." He knelt down at one side of the table. "How many did you have?"

"What a question to ask."

He grinned. "Ah, she's back to normal."

She winced. "Oh, no, I've taken your chair," she groaned, and started to rise.

His hand on her arm stopped her. "Stay," he said. "Please." He got up and drew the bed alongside the table, and sat down on that.

"Don't misconstrue this," he said.

"Then you shouldn't have told me not to misconstrue it." She took a sip of coffee. It burned her tongue and the back of her throat, but she took another sip anyway. "Five," she said. "I think."

She felt her strength returning. She had returned to the hut. Her mind, clouded at first, had cleared. She was here with a man who had fought what he could of her demons, when he might have tried to take advantage of her moment of weakness. He had touched her, but he had not meant to. Her right breast retained the memory of contact with his arm. His . . . bicep. The muscle hard as teak, to hold her up. To keep her from falling.

"You're smiling," he said.

"Am I? Yes, I guess I am."

She spotted a notepad on the table. The pad he had been scrawling in, or drawing in, the night before. She touched fingertips to it, while looking at his face for signs of emotion. Were the contents private? He said nothing. Was that an invitation to look? The pad was there, out in the open, where she or anyone might see it. Did he expect her to ignore it?

She slid it toward her. He did not object.

She flipped it open. The first page was blank.

The second page bore a sketched likeness of her, sitting at the table in the corner. She had been made beautiful by his hand, but the dark, straight lines that formed her spine and her thighs where they came in contact with the wall and bench made her look dangerous. Had she not known the image to be herself, she would have thought her a woman of mystery and intrigue.

He could see that *in her? He could capture it with just a pencil?*

She closed the notepad. "Just who are you?" she asked, her right hand dropping to her lap, closer to her sidearm. "How did you know I would be at the tavern?"

He sat back, looking reflective. "Maybe the better question is: Who are you?" he said. "You handle a sidearm as if you know how to use it, and when not to. Earlier you had every chance—and even a right—to use yours, and yet you held back, employing only the threat of it. You walk as if you have a knife stuck down your right boot."

Her brow knotted. "You could tell that by the way I walk?"

"I could tell something there slightly affected your stride," he replied. "I thought a knife the most likely object, all things considered. For instance, that necklace you have on. There's no reason for you to wear it for this visit, unless it sees double duty as something else. To bind with, maybe? Or to strangle?"

She tightened her grip around the butt of the Kreisler.

"Last evening, at the tavern," he went on, "you sat with your back to a corner, watching everyone who entered—."

"So did you," she blurted.

"I was looking for an inspiration to draw," he said. "Who were you looking for?"

Who, she noted, *not what.*

She decided to test him. "My name is Yoelin Thibbony," she said.

His eyes widened fractionally. "Of the Cargo Transport Thibbonies?" he said. "Dare I inquire: the missing heiress?"

For just a moment her mind darkened. But she had already passed through the worst her return to Havelox Rest might offer. Passed through it with *his help*, she recalled.

Her fingertips caressed the cover of the notepad. "Not," she said, "exactly, no."

"That sounds like a story I'd like to hear."

No, she thought, *you wouldn't. And I'll never know you well enough to tell it to you.*

She released her grasp of the sidearm. Aloud, she said, "Your turn."

"I didn't mean to offend you," he said. "No questions asked. I'm sorry."

She had a ready smile for him. "I won't have you thrown into Squabble Lake," she promised. "So, then?"

"I'm an artist." With a touch of sadness in his tone, he added, "Of the so-called starving variety, in fact. You won't have heard of me."

She turned her hand palm-up on the notepad. "Try me."

"Stefan Coppenrath," he said, and lofted an eyebrow at her.

She gazed at him for a long moment.

"Copper?" she said at last.

His eyes widened as if in shock, and he nodded.

***

The coffee had cooled; Yoelin took a sip, more to conceal her puzzlement than because she needed the jolt. So he was the artist who signed himself Copper, in copper oil on his canvases. Dannik Exeter's collection included one of his portraits, of a young girl walking through shafts of sunlight in a spring wood, but she could not tell him that without revealing her connection to Corporate Security. But what other reason had she for familiarity with his work? Canvas artists were known mostly to family and a few friends; most artists, even obscure ones, worked in holographics.

"I was browsing some art listings, and saw several of yours," she lied.

"But you didn't buy one," said Coppenrath. "Not under your own name, at least."

"No." She regarded him over the rim of the coffee mug. "I don't collect, and most of the time I live aboard my 'skiff."

"Pity. Some of my early work commands a good price. I'm curious: why would you remember me at all?"

She shrugged. "Just something about the name."

"I wanted a name people could lock onto."

"I think Stefan suits you just fine." She set the mug down. "So you make do with canvas and oils, rather than a projector."

His countenance darkened for just an instant, and she was sure she had inadvertently prodded a sensitive spot with him. Then he said, pleasantly enough, "It's a little early in the relationship for me to climb onto my stage and pontificate," he said.

"Relationship?"

He held up his hands. "Oh, no, wrong word. I apologize. Sorry. Quick change of subject indicated here, and I've no idea where to turn. Help?"

She laughed. "Okay . . . okay, earlier you referred to my hut as 'the old place.' Did you live there once?"

"A long time ago, when I was eleven, twelve."

She frowned. "So why didn't you lease it instead?"

"Oh. Why this place. It's . . ."

He turned slightly to gaze out the window. She let him have his silence. She had her own reasons for wanting to lease this hut, reasons she was even less willing to divulge to him than he apparently was to her.

To her surprise, he turned back to her and said, "It's the girl."

Immediately Yoelin's heart stuttered. She fought against the urge to put her hand over it, to calm it. Her face warmed; she hoped the shadows where she was sitting would shelter her.

Gradually his words filtered back to her. ". . . looking for a clue, any clue, as to who she is. Or was. I say 'was.' But I can't see her that way, in the past tense. She's still alive. That's the only way I can see her. That's why she's in most of my early work, the stuff that sells. That's how I see her."

"You said," she began, and stopped, her voice hollow. She took a gulp of coffee and tried again. "You said early work. What about the later pieces?"

He gave her a sheepish grin. "I got away from my themes," he admitted. "I tried to expand my vision. It's funny, but with each canvas that didn't include her, I could see her face, her expression of disapproval. It's crazy, I know. She has no idea who I am. She never did; we never actually met. I only saw her a few times, before . . ."

She swallowed a lump that had just formed in her throat. "Before?" she asked.

"Well, we moved away," he said. "I was twelve at the time.

52

Maybe she was ten."

Nine, she thought.

"It was ten years before I came back here, and by then she was gone. There was some dark business, I learned that much. But of course I could not inquire too closely, not on this planet. I did find out her name."

Ye gods.

"And it was?" she pressed, heart momentarily stilled in anticipation.

"Deirdre Hanratty." He sighed, and added, "A real Deirdre of the Sorrows, with all that happened to that family and to her. The Hanratties was Irish itinerants, like the Wild Geese, I think. I've no idea how or why they wound up here. Anyway, for each of the past five years now I've come back here to spend a month or so, looking for clues and finding none." He paused for a long sigh before continuing, subdued. "And trying to recapture whatever it is that I've lost, and failing even that. But you helped."

That startled her. She braved the question. "How?"

"Last night, at the tavern." He reached out and touched the notepad. "That's the first satisfactory sketch I've done in years." He withdrew his hand. "But it's only a sketch. I'd love to have you to sit for me sometime." Very quickly he added, "If it's not too forward of me to suggest that."

She blanked her expression. "You mean naked?"

"We artists prefer the word 'nude.' But no, with clothes on. What you're wearing now would be okay."

"I'll . . . have to think about that."

"Reporting."

"Was that your communicator?" asked Stefan.

Thank you, Abby. Thank you thank you thank you.

"Stand by, Abby. I'll be with you presently." She got to her feet. "I . . . have to take this," she said, and waved half-heartedly at the door. "It's . . . business."

He stood up. "I suppose I shouldn't ask what kind of business, but . . ." He hesitated. "I'd like to . . . see you again."

You'd better. You've provoked a host of questions.

53

"I don't know if I'd sit for you," she said. "But you can buy me a drink this evening."

He nodded, and she left, not knowing what else to say.

007

Yoelin waited until she was sitting at the table in her own hut before she raised Abby again. Even after the quarter-hour walk back, she continued to feel relieved by the computer's interruption. She'd managed to conceal most of her feelings and reactions from Stefan— or so she hoped—but she was becoming pleasantly uncomfortable in his presence. If she was not careful . . .

"*No.*" She shook her head violently, swinging still-damp black tresses from one shoulder to the other and back. "No, I'm not here for that. I'm not here for you."

"*Shall I leave, then?*"

She chuckled. "Stay, Abby. What do you have for me?"

"*Two commos between Runchal and his middle son, Everhard. Shall I summarize, or do you wish to hear the playback?*"

"Summary first."

"*A woman leasing a hut on Owlhowl Island had asked that another boat be brought out to her, the one she leased being inoperative. She needed it to go to the Spaceport tomorrow. Everhard replaced the boat.*"

Yoelin considered this. "Was there any mention of why she wanted to go to the Spaceport tomorrow?"

"*No. Nor was I able to extrapolate that information.*"

"Owlhowl Island," she mused. "That's about thirty kilometers northwest of here."

She made a face, and shook her head. On other Rescues, she would simply have checked out the island from orbit, obtained lease records, monitored transmissions, and even reconnoitered the hut and its occupant. On Havelox Rest, any of those actions risked her feeding the catfish. Circumspect investigation could resolve only so much, and sheer luck was unreliable.

"Continue monitoring, Abby. Was there a voiceprint for Manohra Dhu among the documents Exeter sent?"

"*No. I calculate a seventy . . . it is probable that Manohra Dhu was able to delete many of her personnel records before she came here. I also calculate the odds that the woman on Owlhowl Island is Dhu as . . . slim."*

She laughed. "Well-calculated. Abby, you said 'many.' So not all of her records were deleted—obviously, since Exeter sent us these. Are there any other records of her still in existence? Records she wouldn't know about, or didn't know how to track down?"

"Do you wish me to conduct a search? It could take some time."

"If you would, please."

"Searching."

Yoelin started to speak, and was stopped by a voice from outside. "Hallo in the hut. Is it safe to approach?"

Sidearm in hand, she scrambled to her feet and rushed to the door, coming to a halt just to one side of it. "Stefan?" she called back.

"I'm not armed."

She cracked the door. He was standing in the sunlight, a few meters from shore—in plain view, as if he had chosen the spot deliberately for that reason. He was still wearing the jeans and the undershirt, and he still looked fit. She pushed the door open and took a step outside, the Kreisler still aimed in his general direction. He raised his hands. His left held a thermal canteen; his right clutched an object she did not recognize, but which seemed to consist of a hollow white cylinder and some sort of handle.

He said, "Excessive wariness does not bode well for our . . . I suppose if I said 'relationship,' you'd shoot me."

She shook her head. "I'd hate to waste the energy beam," she told him. "Why don't you take a few steps closer, so I can be sure I won't miss you."

Stefan obeyed without hesitation, and lowered his hands.

"What is that?" she asked, as he drew within a couple paces.

"You left before you could dry your hair," he explained. He glanced down at her sidearm, and added, "If this is a bad time, I'll leave."

She put the weapon away and backed into the hut, giving him room to enter.

"I know this is most irregular," he said, following her.

"That's a hair dryer?"

"No, it's a canteen; it contains hot coffee."

She made a little sound of exasperation. "In your *other* hand."

"That's an oil dryer. Would you care to sit down?"

"Why?"

He just looked at her as he set the canteen on the table.

"*You're* going to dry my hair?" she asked, and shook her head. "I prefer to—."

Shut up, Yoelin. Shut up shut up shut up.

She made a little gesture toward the chair. "I'll just sit down," she said, and did so, clumsily feeling her way, her eyes on him.

He tucked the dryer under his arm, and moved in behind her. She leaned forward at his gentle nudge, and felt him gather up her hair into one bundle. As he drew it clear, she leaned against the chair and tilted her head back, so that her hair would hang free. She heard a faint *whirr* as he clicked on the dryer. Light tugs said he was liberating a clutch of tresses from the main mass. She closed her eyes. She could tell by the changes in sound that he was waving the dryer back and forth over her hair. Warmth began to seep into her skin. From time to time the back of his free hand brushed against her neck, his tiny hairs catching on hers. She was certain the contact was inadvertent, but each touch invested her with a warmth not unlike that from the dryer, though it came from within.

Moments later she realized he had begun to talk to her, and wondered what she had missed.

". . . while for oils to dry, but the inspiration often remains fresh, and demands attention lest it be lost. The problem with painting over still-wet oils is that the colors tend to mix, to blend. Of course, oils never completely dry, but anyway, I dry the oils I've already applied, to speed up the crusting process, and paint over . . ."

She started. She had drifted off, dozed off, to the sound of his voice. His hand still worked her hair, the overall sensation pleasant, the *whirr* hypnotic. He was standing so close that she could sense his warmth comingling with hers. He smelled like oil paint—cadmium red, she imagined, with a light laugh. He also smelled like resin, and of a walk in the woods. She pictured his bare shoulders, a patina of sweat glistening on his tanned skin whenever he passed through sunlight. Earlier he had protected her. She did not need his protection . . . but she would not mind the attempt. Not mind it at all. He was handling her hair as though it were spun glass, as if she were a canvas and he had in his hand the softest of brushes daubed with the most delicate oil. She would sit for him. He could paint her. He could even paint *her*. She would—.

Vulnerability sprouted within her, and she stiffened, leaning forward to pull away from him.

He drew back, shutting off the dryer. "I'm sorry. I'll be quiet."

Her breathing came shallow, in rapid gasps. The fingers of her right hand had curled around the butt of the Kreisler. After a few more breaths, she reseated the weapon. She allowed a moment for her respiration to return to normal, and said, "It's not . . . not that. And please, stop apologizing."

"Sorry. Uh . . . right, well. Did I hurt you?"

She looked at him over her shoulder. "Ye gods, no, you didn't hurt me. Quite the contrary." She cleared her throat. *Very much the contrary.*

"I didn't mean . . ."

Let me know when you do.

Did I just say that?

She let her hair fall free again. Moments later, he still had not resumed drying it. Puzzled, she looked at him once more. "It's still damp," she reminded him.

He shook his head, and eased back toward the door. "No, I didn't think this through," he said. "I'm losing my . . ."

He pushed the door open, and left.

For a long moment Yoelin sat in the chair, her body twisted so that she might see the doorway. Deep in the background she could hear his fading footsteps crush dried vegetation. He wasn't running, but he was retreating very quickly.

She wondered what she had done to drive him away.

He had intimated that the problem belonged to him. That might be so, but she had no doubt she was at the heart of it. The sketch from last night was proof enough of that.

He had promised to buy her a drink tonight.   She hoped, desperately now, that he would keep it.

Finally she chuckled. "Artists," she muttered.

At least he left her the canteen of hot coffee.

008

Clear thoughts returned to Yoelin halfway through her second mug from the thermos. In the middle of a Rescue she had allowed her feelings to intrude into her actions. Not that there was anything wrong with Stefan—he was exactly the sort of person she would be on the lookout for if she felt inclined toward an interlude. But she rarely encountered such individuals while she was actively engaged—or at any other time, for that matter. He had intruded upon her unexpectedly.

But an *artist?*

And not just that, but an old-fashioned one, who worked in oils, who sketched in graphite, when virtually everyone else in the field had fallen prey to technology. What kind of person did that?

Someone, she decided, who had a different vision.

Someone like Paul Wroclawski? The name leaked through from her past. Silently she admonished herself. *You promised not to think of him.*

She sat back, stunned. She had banished him from her memory, because it hurt too much to remember him. But was the vision he represented correct? Would it take an uncommon perspective for her to find Manohra Dhu?

"Okay, let's examine what we have," she said, and discovered that she was speaking as if Stefan were sitting across the table from her. "On the surface, we're looking for a cube rat who got her hands on files and information normally not privy to her. She has no special skills on record. Aside from one factor, she's as ordinary as sky.

"I said 'on record.' Her history goes back five years. Beyond that, she does not exist. That could mean she is Special Ops, or one of the covert security services. It could mean she has a friend in high places who has created a legend just for her. Lastly, it could mean she has created herself and her own legend, just like I did.

"Which leaves us with two questions. First, why steal corporate territorial archives? And two, why the hell bring them *here?*"

"She is meeting someone."

Yoelin nodded. "That's my guess, too, Abby. But again, all this is from an ordinary perspective. Look at it this way. If this Rescue were on the level, this is exactly how I—or most any other investigator— would approach a resolution. So what if we look at it from some other angle?"

She took a gulp of coffee. It was slightly bitter, as if the grounds had been cut with ground almonds—a common Food Corporation practice. She made a mental note to give Stefan some of the shade-grown Timor beans she had smuggled from Earth. With the fresh reminder of him, in the context of her musings with regard to Dhu, she rubbed the knuckle of her index finger against the tip of her nose, thinking hard. She did not question his artistic abilities, not after seeing that sketch of herself. But what if drawing were, for him, merely a diversion from his primary function?

Which would be what?

"I wonder," she said.

What if other operatives had been dispatched to retrieve the archives? Exeter had not said anything about that—*and she had not asked!*

"Stupid," she said, and bumped the top of the table with her fist.

The name of Stefan Coppenrath was obscure enough to make it unlikely that "Stefan" would encounter anyone who knew the real Coppenrath, especially on Havelox Rest. She recalled that her acknowledgement had taken him aback, if very briefly.

Following that line, was Manohra Dhu the woman's real name? It seemed unlikely, given her lack of history under it. But did the name, like her own, have an origin?

Even with the question, her mood darkened. A memory sprang free and flew about in her mind, cackling. She tried to swat at it, but already she saw herself once again inside the crate.

***

The crate smelled mostly of raw wood and urine. Some of the stench escaped through the two knotholes she had punched out, but most of it hung inside like an evil fog. There was also an animal smell, especially on the wood, where she had found tufts of hair among the splinters. Some of those splinters had made their way into her skin, where they now itched.

The crate itself trembled whenever the ship's engines kicked in, and bestirred her awake. In the darkness, she had lost all sense of time, but surely several days had passed since her father had sold her in a futile attempt to forestall collection on his debts. Since a man had taken her aside by the arm, to watch while the others killed . . .

Tears welled once more.

The words she had heard meant little. Gambling debts. Her father shouting, then pleading, finally whimpering. Her mother shrieking, and running outside. Blue beams searing her parents, scorching them.

In the dark, she rubbed her arms, sore where the man had clutched her, sore before that where her father had struck her, angry and fearful. He had always been angry and fearful, especially when he smelled of ale. But he had promised they would be safe on Havelox Rest.

He had also promised not to hit her anymore.

But he had hit her. And they had not been safe.

There had been no one around to help her. Even those whose duty it was to help her, had yielded instead to the evil she faced. She had no one to turn to.

"Let Malik have her," the man holding her had said. "He'll pay good money."

"Ship her," another had said.

And they had thrown her into the crate, and nailed it shut, leaving only a thin opening through which food and water might be inserted.

She had just turned ten . . .

***

Yoelin emerged shaken from the memory. The coffee in the mug rippled—a tear had fallen from the tip of her nose. She felt another coalesce, and drop. The coffee was cold to her taste, and she pushed the mug aside. The slow realization that she had scored a minor victory brightened her outlook; this time revisiting a segment of her past had not nauseated her.

She glanced around the hut. "Do something," she growled at herself.

Her mind went blank. She looked at the table and the automatic pistol without seeing them. Dismay swept over her, and she gave a little cry, as the needs of the weapon dawned on her. Swiftly she disassembled the pistol, and cleaned and oiled it. Following reassembly, she slapped the magazine back into the butt and set the safety. Finally, she stood up, equipped and armed herself, and slipped the Palmetto into a pocket of her jeans.

Upon leaving the hut, she half-expected to see Stefan, and knew a moment's disappointment as she saw that the way to the *Betha* tied up at the pier was unimpeded. She made her way down to it, noting ruefully the scuff marks in the dirt where she had fallen the night before. After untying the mooring line, she climbed aboard, started the motor, and set out on a leisurely course for the dock at the Spaceport.

Arriving half an hour later, she boarded the *Sequana*, resupplied herself with clothing and food, and returned to the boat, ignoring the curious looks she received from the douane personnel by the Port Authority station. After a few moments, she rounded the cape and the tavern, and headed out to sea, setting a course for Owlhowl Island.

***

The green water of the open sea reminded her of Stefan's eyes. Overhead the sky was clear, with orange Karsh bleeding its midday light onto the water. The star reminded her of a great, overripe fruit. Her royal blue pullover was now indigo where occasional wafts of spray and froth striped her. The wet fabric chilled her when it came in contact with her skin, but she quickly grew accustomed to it. Seated on the aft bench, she slowed the *Betha*'s speed to smooth the ride, then locked the tiller and set the automatic compass.

Two hours to Owlhowl, she thought, as she surveyed the open sea. Behind her, Birdfoot Island gradually shrank to a few teeth protruding up from the forested hump. Almost even with her now, a small clump of warped sedimentary rock stood guard several kilometers north of Birdfoot. She studied the waterproof charts and found that the islet was named Inaccessible, and she soon understood why. The terrain lines around the coast were almost superimposed on one another.

Owlhowl Island, on the other hand, consisted of shallow valleys northwest and southeast of a series of long, narrow hills, almost like eskers, if glaciers had once covered the land. The features suggested that the huts might easily be spotted, unless there were intervening woods. The island did not seem a likely place for someone on the run to hide out, even under the protections of the Havelock traditions.

She glanced around, and back over her shoulders. As far as she could determine visually, she was not being followed. That disappointed her.

What did I do, Stefan? Or was it something I said?

He had departed at an awkward moment that had been steadily growing in intensity. Much more of that hair-drying, and she would have . . .

"What?" she chided herself. "What would you have done? Pitched him onto the bed?" She sighed. "Besides, I'm part of his past. I'm his muse, and I can never tell him that." After pondering that for a moment, she shook her head sadly. "It's better this way."

Liar!

A dark smear in the distance gradually resolved itself into an island. As yet she could not make out any specific features, or detect white-capped breakers at the shoreline. The island so far was just a blob, an obstacle between herself and points north. Slightly off-course, she made a helm adjustment.

Something solid struck the underside of the boat.

It had enough impact to worry her. Nothing in her earlier memories warned her of large aquatic predators. As a child, she had often swum in the lagoons, her toes tickled occasionally by little pink and blue fish. Larger fish—more precisely, fish analogs—inhabited the seas, but aside from a few fillets brought home by her parents, she had never seen any.

She saw a splash off the port bow, and something glistening and grayish brown looped at the water's surface. Another bump yawed the *Betha* to starboard, and badly off-course. She drew the Kreisler and held it ready.

It rose alongside the boat like a cobra, about a meter out of the water. An eel, Yoelin guessed, or a prehistoric sea serpent. Seeing the double rows of flat-edged teeth in its open mouth, she withheld fire. The thing was herbivorous, and probably fed on algae. It eyed her briefly as if it were curious, nothing more.

"Well, hello there," she said.

The creature just looked at her.

She reached into a plastic pouch and came up with a chunk of dried fruit. After holding it up for display, she tossed it into the open mouth. The creature's head drew back as if it were surprised. Then it closed its mouth around the chunk and sank beneath the choppy waters, to her sigh of relief.

She did not relax, but returned to course and accelerated. Herbivorous it might be, but if it slung itself aboard, it might sink the boat. She had no idea how long the creature was, but if snakes offered a proper comparison by being able to rise or strike a third of their body length, then this one probably reached at least five meters, as water offered far less support than land.

After a minute or so of higher speed she slowed the boat, and looked back. The sea was clear, which meant nothing; it had been clear at the first collision.

"I hope you're not the runt of the family," she muttered.

In the distance, whitecaps marked the shallows along the beach. She dug out the chart again and saw that the indented southern coast of Owlhowl Island formed a sort of bight, less than two kilometers wide, the shoreline broken by a number of shallow coves, none protected by sand bars. Inlets like tooth marks indented the rest of the island's perimeter. But the chart did not indicate places of habitation. She would have to locate those visually.

Although she had anticipated difficulties in finding the woman who had requested the new boat, she grimaced at having to trust to chance. Unable to ask direct questions, she had no other option.

The shoreline was clearly visible now. Piers protruded into the mild surf, and several boats bobbed where they were tied up. Further ashore, she caught sight of several rude dwellings, but no one was about, and it was impossible to determine which ones, if any, were occupied. She swung the boat around to starboard and began a circumnavigation of the island, hoping—but not expecting—to catch sight of Manohra Dhu.

The journey around the island proved unproductive, the dwellings and piers scattered on the leeward curve, all but non-existent on the windward. Although the island was a mere two kilometers across in its greatest dimension, she did not see any human activity in the interior, even with field glasses. She did notice some cattle and sheep, and something that she estimated at the size of a pig shuffling through some shrubbery. Plus the usual chickens, and even a couple of geese. But no golden-skinned, dark-haired female denizens.

At least the journey got her out of the hut.

After she rounded the western cape that marked the boundary of the island's bight, she spotted someone walking on one of the piers. A man, dressed casually, with brown hair and tanned skin. Not a long-time resident, then, she concluded. Feeble Karsh made tanning difficult. She banked the *Betha* toward the pier, while the man came to a stop, poised as if waiting for her to arrive.

Even as Yoelin wondered what reason she might give for her visit, one occurred to her. She pulled up to the pier next to the man, but remained seated in the boat. This close to him, she now noticed a vertical jagged scar alongside his right temple; the old injury jogged a memory, and she thought she might have seen him before. When nothing came to her, she shook off the notion; thousands of men doubtless had such scars on their faces.

After his nod and brief smile, Yoelin said, "I heard there was a boat out here in need of repair."

"And I suppose you're a mechanic," the man said, his tone laden with doubt.

"If it's the engine, I can probably fix it," she said, and spread her hands in a mild plea. "Hey, I'm just looking for some work."

The man gazed out to sea for a few moments. Finally he said, "They brought a new boat out."

She nodded. "I was afraid of that. Still, perhaps I should talk to whoever leased it. If the problem was the operator's fault, perhaps I can earn a spot of dosh for some advice." She made a show of looking up and down the shoreline. "Which one is he?"

"It's a she. And she's not here." He spun on his heel, and headed back to shore.

Hello and goodbye.

She turned the boat away and headed back out to sea. Already the feeling had arrived that she had pressed her luck just a little too far, and that her queries might be reported. She doubted the consequences would involve digestion; at most, a caution regarding privacy. Still, she would have to tread lightly.

The great eel—for so she had decided to regard the creature—did not make another appearance during her return journey, nor did any of its relatives. At one point, for a few seconds, she saw the water roil off her starboard bow, but nothing more. A shoal of fish, perhaps, or even a seamount, though none was listed on the chart. But no great eel. She would ask Stefan about it when she saw him at *The Rutting Skull*.

If she saw him.

No, it had to be *when*. It just *had to* be.

She recalled a song from long ago, one of the classics. She couldn't recall the name of the singer. Abby would know it, but it wasn't the singer who mattered at the moment. It was the song.

I've got to see you again.

009

Seated once again at her corner table, Yoelin waited in the tavern for Stefan to arrive. Darkness proceeded from dusk and twilight without her leave; she had feared the moment was rushing onward when she would realize, at last, that he was not coming. If dusk remained, so did hope. But if darkness fell . . .

It fell, and she could not stop it.

Only the light from the tavern fusion globes in the open rafters kept her hopes alive. Feeble light, as if Karsh itself were the inspiration. Feeble hopes.

Melancholy set in. She nursed her second ale, intending it for her last. The alcohol was slow to take effect, for she had already taken a repast of Tuscan salami and a small salad with a drizzle of olive oil. But solitude had much the same effect as ale; she found herself on the verge of brooding.

The door opened, lifting her hopes before two men entered the tavern to shoot them down. Evidently they had been fishing, to judge from the few snatches of their conversation that reached her. She added them to the periphery of her awareness; they were not Stefan.

Stefan, who had seen her *before*.

She had gotten no sense that he had caught even a glimmer of who she was. Who she had been. Many little girls with long, dark hair grew into tall women with long, dark hair. But sooner or later, if their on-again, off-again "relationship" continued, questions about her past might occur to him. Should she tell him, or let him figure it out on his own? But if she opted for the latter, would he be angry when he realized she had known all along? What was the risk? More importantly, what was *at* risk?

She took a sip of ale, still in nursing mode.

No, Stefan was out of luck, looking for Deirdre Hanratty. That girl was dead. She had died the moment she emerged from the crate.

***

They shoved food through the slot. In a bowl. It looked like the oatmeal her parents sometimes prepared for breakfast, except this was cold. They did not give her a spoon; she ate by scooping the stuff out of the bowl with her fingers and cramming it into her mouth. At first she had refused to eat, but hunger soon overcame her revulsion at the slimy gray-brown mass in the bowl.

Perhaps it was the sixth day of her captivity, or the seventh. She had no way of counting, and no desire to do so, for time had lost meaning for her. She was fed, she did her evacuations in a corner, and she slept. She passed through stages of emotions, although she did not identify them at the time, but simply experienced them. Terror, fear, despondence.

Anger.

Finally, rage.

She had noted that the ship stopped several times during her transportation. Sometimes she heard the sound of a door opening, of machinery. Cargo was being loaded, or unloaded. She heard indistinct voices. On the first few occasions, she called out for help, but no one came to her rescue, and she soon abandoned those attempts.

When rage arrived, she acted out for a few minutes, pounding on the wood of the crate until splinters embedded in her fists. Frustrated, she sat down, in a shaft of light that poured through one of the knotholes. She decided to see what was out there.

She found only more shipping crates. Some of wood, some of corrugated metal. Various sizes. She seemed to be high up, as if her own crate stood on another. She tried to look straight down, but only at an angle was she able to see the floor. It looked far away, as far as the floor had been when her father had raised her over his head.

It looked far enough for what she had in mind.

She stood against one side of the crate, took a deep breath, and dashed herself against the opposite side. The crate tilted, then settled back down. She tried again, and again, and managed to slide the crate just a little. But not enough. Her shoulder ached where it had struck the wood. She turned so that she might apply the other shoulder. Once more she dashed, and jumped at the last moment, hoping to tip the crate over the edge.

For just a moment the crate hung over the edge . . . and then it gave way. She floated in the air as it fell, and slammed into the wood when it landed. Wood splintered, and cracked, and yielded. She was pelted by fragments whose nature she did not want to think about. The impact left her stunned, and bleeding from a cut on her forehead. Gradually the realization sank in, and gave her hope: I *did* it.

But she was not free. Not yet. The crate was weakened, but still held.

She found a cracked board, and worked it, the broken wood tearing at her fingers. It hurt, and she told herself it didn't hurt, and she believed it. Thrust, pull, and thrust again. The board came free. She might reach through the gap all the way up to her shoulder, if she chose. If she could work one more board loose . . .

A door opened. More lights came on. She heard footsteps, and muffled voices. She heard her own heartbeat. Her breathing rasped, as if something was caught in her throat, and she threw a bloody hand over her mouth to stop the sound.

Don't let them find me.

She held her breath.

If they found her, and saw what she had done, what would they do? She did not know. She knew only that she was being shipped to Malik. The man who had a use for young girls. She wasn't quite sure what that meant, but she was absolutely certain she did not want to find out.

Footsteps. They seemed to be quieter now, as if whoever made them were moving away from her.

One or two lights went out.

A door closed.

She exhaled in a long moan, and drew an equally long but squeaky breath. Several rapid, shallow breaths followed this one, until she could no longer feel her heart pound.

One more board.

She hit it. She laid down and kicked at it, and hurt her heel. The pain did not matter. Only escape mattered. She kicked again, and felt wood give. She kicked the middle of the board, and saw it crack. Another kick splintered it. She got up and pushed at the two halves and pulled at them and worked them loose. And cast them aside.

Squeezed through the opening. Jagged edges tore at her soiled tunic. Thrust herself through.

She was free.

Standing outside the crate now, she inspected it with an iron detachment, for it could no longer imprison her. Stenciled in the wood in black block letters were the words Thibbony Cargo Transport. She saw nothing to indicate origin or destination. She walked around the ruptured crate, looking for more markings, but found nothing. The door was still secured with a lock. A hasp, a metal loop. A simple enough device. She turned the lock over and read the name of the manufacturer. Yoelin Lock Company.

One day, she meant to have a word with them.

But first, she had to get out of the ship's cargo hold.
***

The voice drew her back. "Are you all right, mum?"

Yoelin looked up blankly from her mug. One of Runchal's daughters came into focus, this one with short red hair. Wearing a simple frock and leggings. Yoelin did not recall the girl's name, and perhaps had not even known it. She nodded, and looked away, dismissing her.

What is wrong with me?

Briefly she reviewed the past two days. Her security awareness had faltered. Proximity to the dreaded place of her childhood had shaken her, and for a few moments she had succumbed to the nightmare. Still, overall, she had proven herself stronger on this visit, and recovered quickly. That was something. On the other hand, she had undergone the experience in the presence of a relative stranger, and her mental defenses had deserted her. Worse, she had allowed that stranger to get his foot in the door of her life, in effect throwing her usual caution to the wind. Worst of all, she wanted him there, and she hardly knew anything about him. He might be an artist; so was the Marquis de Sade.

She wondered how much of her negative and defensive feelings stemmed from anxiety. She cast a glance across the open bay. The table in the opposite corner was still empty. Stefan had not shown.

Again the door opened, to admit an older couple. The pair wandered to the bar, pausing along the way to greet someone they knew. Two or three other people waved to them.

Long-term residents, she concluded, fortifying herself with another slug of ale. *Something I can never be.*

She glanced toward the door; it had not closed. In the opening stood Stefan, gazing at her as if she were the only person in the tavern.

She felt a tear well in each eye, and had no idea why. She did not bother to brush them away.

He allowed the door to close behind him, and approached her table as if she had thrown him a rope and was pulling him toward her. Without invitation, he sat down across the table from her. Just out of her reach, the separation saying that he had measured her and found himself uncertain with regard to the nature of her greeting.

"I was painting," he said, as if it explained everything.

She nodded, and found her voice. "I thought it might be something like that."

"No, you didn't."

"No, I didn't," she conceded.

He spoke as if he had rehearsed various sets of words, and had finally selected these. "Over the years, I've received advice from others to the effect that an artist needs to be detached from the objects of his art," he said. "I'm not certain that's the correct approach, but it is the one I have chosen to take. Had chosen to take. Then, while I was drying your hair, I . . ." He paused, his voice grown rusty.

Before he could continue, she said, "You found yourself losing that detachment."

He nodded.

"I felt it, too," she told him. "If that helps."

Silence spilled between them, pregnant with directions for them each to take.

He clasped his hands together on the table, and studied them. She noticed that several of his fingers were flecked with shades of blue. "I don't know what to do," he said, more to himself than to her.

I can think of something.

"But you started a painting," she pointed out.

"I am unable to finish it."

Think of a number between one and, oh, say three or four.

He left an open space after the question, inviting her curiosity. She yielded readily. "Why not?"

"I need you to sit for me."

Sit, stand, lie down, or just clear this table, I don't care how we—

She cut off that thought, afraid it might show in her expression. "You're painting me," she said flatly.

"I don't even know why," he admitted, a touch of complaint in his tone.

"You had an inspiration. Like the sketch last night."

"Yes. Yes, exactly. An inspiration. I haven't . . . not like this, not so strong, not for . . . for years." His eyes bored into hers. "I need you."

Deliberately she expanded the meaning of his statement. "You hardly know anything about me."

"That's where you're wrong."

Her breath caught in her throat. *Ye gods. He knows.*

Her eyes narrowed as she peered at him. *Does he know?*

In her mind, the possibility that she might take him back to her hut for the night now dissipated. "Tell me," she said. It was not a request.

"I looked you up."

Something I should have done, with regard to you.

"And?" she pressed.

"And . . . I'd like to hire you."

Startled, she leaned back, appraising him. *What did he know? What could he want?* He looked sober and serious, his sea-green eyes calm, as if a storm had passed.

"In two capacities," he added.

Her brow furrowed.

"The first is easy," he went on, as if unaware of the effect of his request on her, his voice growing more animated as he spoke. "You have inspired me, I've told you as much. I want you to pose for me, for several canvases. I don't know how many. Maybe it would be a

73

permanent thing, something you would do for a certain period of time each year." He made a series of irregular circles with his hands. "Because I have so many ideas—no, visions—whirling around in me. I see you, as point and counterpoint in those visions. I want to paint you as I see you, not as you are. That's my vision. I can't explain . . ."

Abruptly he brightened, and took a gulp of ale from her mug. "No, wait, I *can* explain. It's why I work in oils, in charcoal, in pastels. If I use technology, I can depict stars, let's say, in dimensions, with depth and perspective, as they are. That's the key phrase: as they are. It's difficult to put a subjective vision into objective technology. Van Gogh could never have composed *Starry Night* in holographics, because the technology could not reproduce his own, personal, particular vision, do you see, Yoelin? Do you see that? Van Gogh painted what *he* saw, not what was. In doing so, he made reality of what he saw. His vision became real. Seurat saw his themes as points of light and color. Monet saw his realities the way Plato thought of them, in that existence itself is but a glimmer of what is real; all we see is an impression, and that is what he gave us. Technology fails true art, Yoelin. Somehow, you've reminded me of this. You've restored my roots. You've given me vision. I've never had anyone, any person, do this to me before." He fell silent for a moment, and added softly, "Except one other."

Yoelin held her breath. She wished she could close her ears. She knew what he was going to say. Or she thought she did.

He took a deep breath and slowly let it out, as if to steady himself. "You have a very quiet presence out there. Either you are a little-known amateur, or—as I believe—a skilled professional. I found your byline readily enough. *Guardian Angel.* When no one else will answer the cry for help, you will. That's your reputation. You protect and defend the weak, and give them strength; you return things that were taken from the helpless; you intervene in one-sided conflicts, you . . . I don't know that a single word or phrase defines what you do. One cry at a time, you answer it."

"What do you want, Stefan?" she whispered, against her will.

"Do you believe in fate, Yoelin?"

She took half a maple cheroot from the pack in her shirt pocket and lit it, exhaling the smoke away from him. "No," she said.

"A wise man once wrote, a long time ago, that the two most important days of your life are—."

She held up her hand. "I know the quote. 'The day you are born, and the day you learn why.' Samuel Clemens. He also said that cauliflower was nothing but cabbage with a university degree. Or words to that effect. So what?"

"You are my Muse."

She pushed her bench back and stood up. Her face warmed. Aware of other eyes on her, she kept her voice down, but spoke fiercely. "*Damn* it, Stefan. I can't be that for you. I can't be what you want."

"It's too late," he said. "You already are. Please, sit down. Please?"

Reluctantly she sat, glaring at him. Unexpected pain made her cry out. The cheroot had slipped in her fingers, and she had caught it at the coal. She dropped the stub on the table, and picked it up further back. This time, after she took a drag, she blew the smoke at him.

He did not blink, or give any sign of discomfort. "The painting I began today is why I was born," he said.

The conviction in his tone took her aback. It reminded her of the way she had felt at the outset of her work. The way she still felt. She wished he had not said this to her; now she had to help him if she could, because now she understood him. And she hadn't even seen the painting yet.

"That is my fate. Encountering you was fated," he went on. "But this is not about the painting. I've already covered your posing for me. No, I also want you to find her. The other one. The girl I told you about. Deirdre Hanratty. If she's dead, I want to know what happened to her. If she's alive, I would like to know where she is, and I'll pay additional if you can—."

"Stop," she ordered, half-rising from the bench. The request was unexpected. Understanding him or not, she had just been asked to do the one thing she dared not do, without putting her hard-won psyche at risk. "Just . . . just stop, Stefan. I can't do that. The answer is no."

She settled back onto the bench. "Perhaps I'll sit for you this once, for free. I haven't decided yet. It's even possible that, if I'm not otherwise engaged, I might come sit for you at other times. But I am here . . . for another reason, and I have to focus on it."

"On contract."

She nodded.

"I see." He looked glum, then brightened. "But you will finish it at some point, right?"

"I don't plan ahead, Stefan. In this business, I can't afford to."

"That sounds like you're turning me down in advance."

"I'm a very bad Muse."

He gave her an arch look.

"No, Stefan," she said.

"I thought, earlier, you . . ."

"Earlier, I might have. I might still. But not tonight. I need some time."

"So I should go back to painting."

"That might be best," she said.

He got to his feet. "Should I bring you some coffee in the morning?"

She decided he was testing her welcome mat. "I'll make some for you," she told him.

She watched him walk away. He did not turn back around. She did not know what that meant. Had it been herself leaving, she would have glanced back.

No more complications, she wished, as she downed the rest of her ale. She gave him a five-minute start, then headed out for her own boat.

010

Yoelin came awake instantly, without knowing why. Had someone drawn within ten meters of the hut, Abnoba's sensor array would have sounded the alarm she had placed under her pillow. She slipped it out and glanced at the dial, but it was dark, unactivated. Starlight through the window yielded just enough light for her to perceive shadows inside the hut. Kreisler in hand, she puzzled out the shapes of nothing more ominous than furniture.

Gradually she became aware of the sound of distant splashing. A commotion in the lagoon. For the splashes to reach her ears, the cause would have to be something large. Stefan? But surely he would have called out to her. And why would he be in the lagoon?

She stood up in one swift motion and strode to the door, putting her ear next to it to listen. She thought she heard a cry, ever so faint, like a night bird high overhead, but it might have been her imagination. The splashing itself abated. Weapon ready, she yanked the door open and dove outside, rolling to her feet with her bare skin festooned with flakes of dead leaves and dried bark. Still in a crouch, she whirled around with the Kreisler, seeking targets, finding none. Starlight twinkled in the lagoon, and shimmered as if something were disturbing the surface of the water. Briefly she debated whether to put on some clothes, but whatever was lurking about probably didn't care one way or the other. Her finger touched the illumination function on her sidearm, without turning it on. At the moment, she had good night vision; it seemed a shame to negate it until she had something specific to examine.

After brushing off most of the dead vegetation, she moved carefully toward the shore of the lagoon. She had taken only a few steps when she spied a second boat next to the pier. Again she crouched down and swept the sidearm around her, ready to fire at the slightest movement. The feeling of vulnerability increased her heart rate, and she took a couple of steadying breaths. Her lips puffed out with each exhalation. Nothing came at her out of the dark, nothing moved. A shadow or two momentarily fired her imagination, until she resolved them as harmless boles shifting in the same soft breeze that now chilled her bare skin.

She returned her attention to the second boat while she crept to the pier. Even in the starlight she could see that it was unoccupied. But there seemed to be a dark shape floating in the water beside it. She began to wonder whether it was the sound of the motor that had awakened her. She did not recall hearing anything—probably the operator had coasted toward shore from beyond the shoals.

So where was he?

The question sent a fresh chill across her shoulders. She hunched slightly, as if in anticipation of an impact, while she spun around, seeking a threat, finding none. Her breath caught in her throat, just above her heart. She located the dark shape she had spotted moments earlier. It was bobbing gently with the waves . . . but alongside it was another dark shape, and it was *moving*.

Moving *toward* her.

She stepped back from the edge of the pier and shone the sidearm light at the shape just as it rose from the water like a support post. In the light, a great eel blinked at her and opened its mouth. She almost fired at it in surprise. The spot from the light included the other dark shape. It looked like a man. She focused the light on it . . . on what had been a man.

Consternation shook her. Her breath came in shallow rasps as she illuminated the man's face. The great eel had taken a bite out of his neck, severing tendons and arteries and exposing neck bones. There were tears in his clothing where other bites had relieved him of flesh. She swung the light back to his head. There seemed to be a scar down the left side of his face.

The man from the pier on Owlhowl Island? The face and hair were the same. Clearly he had come here surreptitiously, and therefore most likely with evil intent. But why?

The great eel closed its mouth, and opened it again. It seemed to be waiting for something.

She licked her lips, and found her voice. "Well, hello there."

Once more it closed and opened its mouth.

"I didn't bring you anything," she said. "I'm sorry." Cautiously she moved to the edge of the pier. The great eel approached her. She reached out and touched the top of its head, her fingers giving a scritch to the rough scales there. Though moist, they felt more reptilian than piscine, and for a moment she wondered whether the creature was some kind of dinosaur analog.

Suddenly the great eel emitted a sound like the bark of a large dog, and slapped itself into the water, drenching Yoelin. She sputtered, and drew back, struggling to fathom what the creature was doing. After a moment it reappeared, mouth open. Her head began to ache. She felt an urge come over her, an urge for . . . something sweet.

Her own mouth open in amazement, she stared at the great eel. "You want a-a treat?" she asked, hushed.

Again the mouth closed and opened.

Ye gods. It's telepathic.

She sat down on the pier, the wet wood cold against her skin. Her mind skidded to a halt in disbelief. In the blank space she grasped images of what had happened. The creature waiting for her to appear. The silent approach of the boat. The man with evil intentions. The lunge onto the boat.

The ripping and shredding of flesh. The blood.

She shined the light down at the water. Yes, little fish were already at work on shards of skin and muscle and dark smears of blood in the water. Nature cleaning up. The creature, however, had other sustenance in mind.

She got back to her feet, and held up one finger in what she hoped was the universal signal to wait a moment. With that, she dashed back to the hut, threw on some clothes, and gathered up the Palmetto and the pouch containing dried fruit. When she returned to the pier and sat down in tailor fashion, the great eel was still watching, and waiting.

The survival part of her longed to examine the dead man, and to have Abnoba take a scan and do an identity search. But that would have to wait. There was something winsome about the great eel that reminded her of—of all things—a puppy. And dogs were nothing if not loyal.

She patted the pier, and looked at the creature.

It approached, and rose out of the water, looping itself into a pile of coils beside her. As big around as her waist, it seemed to be about six or seven meters long, and serpentine, with a tail that came to a point. Flippers fore and aft evidently provided locomotion; each was the size of her arm. From what she had just observed, the limbs were primarily functional in water; on the pier they gave only weak support. The body seemed to have an internal but flexible skeleton. The creature's head was mounted on its neck in such a way that a vertical position of the neck did not allow the head to face forward. Instead, it had to bend its neck in a sort of question mark to look at her. It was doing so now; its nose nudged her shoulder. It was like being prodded with a plank.

"Okay, okay," she said, pushing its head back. She dug out a morsel of dried fruit and tossed it into its mouth, now conveniently open. Dimly she wondered what would happen when she ran out of dried fruit.

Her thoughts turned to the creature's activities. Somehow, it had followed her to the lagoon, by scent or by sound, or even by some mental connection. But why? Her random act of kindness? Why hadn't the inhabitants of the planet interacted with these great eels before? While the synopsis of Havelox Rest described aquatic denizens of various sizes in the planet's seas in general terms, it made no specific mention of the eels or their telepathic abilities.

And they weren't eels. She twisted on the pier to face the creature. It raised its head and opened its mouth again, and she fed it a piece of pineapple. The flippers denied it an identity as a snake analog.

"At least I could give you a name," she told it. "Or do you have one already?"

She closed her eyes for a moment, listening for a message. When none came, she opened her eyes again. It was still watching her, but now its mouth was closed.

"Something simple," she mused, and perked up as a name occurred to her. "Ellie? Yes, Ellie sounds right, but I hope you're a girl." She scritchied the scales on top of its head. "Hi, Ellie. I'm Yoelin."

Ellie responded by eyeing the pouch of dried fruit at her feet. She withdrew a chunk and held it out in the palm of her hand. Very gently Ellie tilted her head to one side and picked up the chunk.

"Thanks for coming to my rescue," said Yoelin. "I have some alarms set, but not this far away." She looked up at the sky. "Dawn's almost here. Perhaps you should go back into the water. If someone should see you, they might not understand." She added what she hoped was a mental image of the creature returning to the water.

Ellie gave her knee a little nudge, then slithered back into the lagoon, scarcely making a sound.

Yoelin stood up. In the middle of stretching, she spotted movement at the edge of the woods. Almost immediately the Kreisler was in her hand and aimed. A moment later she recognized Stefan.

Oblivious to her drawn weapon, he stepped and skidded down the slope toward the pier, dislodging stones and clumps of dirt. In the lagoon, water roiled. Yoelin let out a gasp of fear and dashed toward him, meeting him at the base of the pier. The collision knocked him back; she spun around and faced the lagoon, waving her arms.

"*No*, Ellie," she shouted, and tried to conjure the right mental image. "*Friend*. It's okay. He's okay."

She glanced over her shoulder to locate Stefan. He had landed on his rump. As he struggled back to his feet, dusting himself off, he paused when he caught sight of what had just emerged from the water. He cried out an alarm and started to reach for her, but she brushed his arm aside.

"No, don't," she said. "Don't make any move toward me that Ellie might interpret as hostile."

He stared at the lagoon, and the creature whose neck was now a good two meters up out of the water. "Ellie? That thing is an Ellie? And is that another boat?"

Ellie emitted a bark, and slapped the water with her neck. Water washed over the pier. Yoelin took out another piece of fruit and tossed it to her. Yoelin received a sense of pleasure as Ellie caught it, then slipped back into the lagoon. When she had disappeared, Yoelin spun back around, clipping her sidearm.

"What are you doing here?" she demanded.

Stefan still had his eyes on the water. "What . . . *was* that?"

She shoved both hands against his chest, and almost knocked him down again. "Stefan, what did you think you were doing? I could have killed you if I hadn't been down here."

He blinked. "What? Why?"

She sighed, exasperated. "I set proximity alarms," she explained, with forced patience. "They would have gone off if you'd approached the hut, and I might not have been able to hold back my response. Ye gods, Stefan, *let me know* when you're in the area."

"I would have, if I hadn't spotted you down here. What was that thing?"

"I'll tell you later. For the last time, why are you here?"

"Today is market day," he told her. "I thought we could go shopping together."

She stared at him. "It's what day?"

"Every ten days a cargo cruiser stops by, making the rounds, and they set up a market at the Spaceport for people to buy food, clothing, necessities, luxuries . . . I thought you knew this. Anyway, today's the day."

She felt dubious. "A market."

"A big one, usually. Over a hundred stalls and kiosks. Just about the entire population of Rest will be there, all three thousand of them. That's why we want to arrive early: we'll want to dock the boat as close as we can."

"A market?" she repeated.

"You said that."

She shook her head, and waved him off. Her excitement grew as she thought, *No, she enjoys markets. I saw her in the hologram.* "*That's* where she'll be," she blurted. The impulse to kiss him on the cheek startled her. She fought it back.

You're as giddy as a schoolgirl. Cease and desist!

"What are you talking about?" asked Stefan, confusion in his tone. "Where *who* will be?"

Suddenly he grabbed her arm, and she turned into him,

beginning a defensive maneuver that would end with him sprawled on the pier. At the last second she held back. He was staring hard at the lagoon, not at her, and pointing.

"That's . . . a body," he gulped.

She stepped away. "Yes, I know."

"But—."

"I don't know who he is, or why he came here," she told him. "Not exactly, anyway."

He seemed to mull that over. "Ellie?"

"She seems to have assigned herself to my protection."

"But what are we going to do?" he asked.

"I'll handle it."

"But—."

"I'll handle it, Stefan." Softening, she added, "It's my kind of business."

She gazed out at the lagoon and nodded to herself. The idyllic interlude on Havelox Rest had ended when the scar-faced man had shown up at her pier. Something about the terms of this contract was not as it had been presented to her. With that thought, she cast a sidelong glance at Stefan. Was he simply an artist? Certainly he could draw. If the persona he had offered her was an artifice, he was making one hell of a good job of it. But now she had to hold suspicion in the back of her mind. No giddiness. No impulses.

She drew a deep breath and sighed. *Damn.*

011

Yoelin searched the second boat, without turning up anything that might give a clue as to the dead man's purpose. After recording his DNA and the remains of his face for an identity check, she towed the body and the boat out to sea, with Stefan fretting all the while, and left them there. She had no doubt that the aquatic denizens would dispose of the body. The boat would be found; she even considered taking it back to the dock on the pretext of having found it adrift, and decided against it. If the man had accomplices, she did not want them to connect her to the boat, as surely would happen if she reported the derelict.

"But who was he?" pressed Stefan, seated on the aft bench. "What did he want? And what was that creature, that Ellie?"

Yoelin gazed past him at the sea. Thus far there had been no sign of the creature, and she hoped that would continue. Briefly she considered how much information to reveal to Stefan. If he were an operative in deep cover, he would already be aware of her mission. But if he was merely ingenuous, as he appeared . . . it might not hurt to have an ally.

She put the *Betha* on autopilot and sat down on the middle bench, facing him. "I don't know who he was," she said, her voice just audible above the rush of air and the breath of the motor. "I've engaged Abnoba to search for him based on DNA and facial ident. In fact, I'm surprised she hasn't already pinged me with some information."

"You'd have to have a high security clearance to be able to go that deep," said Stefan.

"I do." Her eyes narrowed. "But how would you know what I'd need?"

He shrugged. "It's an integral part of my profession," he replied. "In order to paint what I see, I have to have a wide range of knowledge. It doesn't make me an expert in any particular field; it simply rounds me out."

"Considering the stealth of his arrival, I've concluded that he was going to try to kill me," she went on. "I don't know why. I ran into him earlier on Owlhowl Island, where I made a casual inquiry about a boat repair job. It was clear he knew the individual in question, and equally clear he didn't want to discuss the matter."

"And the individual in question?"

Yoelin took out Abnoba and projected the market scene hologram of Dhu just above the deck. "Assuming he and I were talking about the same person, this is she," she explained. "She was going under the name Manohra Dhu. She stole some official documents. Corporatia wants them and her back."

"Suppose she doesn't want to go back?" said Stefan. "Runchal isn't going to allow you to simply abduct her."

"I haven't worked that out yet. I haven't even established that Dhu is in fact here on Rest. But for the fee I'm being paid, if fulfilling the terms of my contract means never being able to return here, I'll risk it."

"Are you going to kill her?"

She shut off the hologram and stared hard at him. "I cannot be hired to kill someone, Stefan," she said, with some asperity. "I might have to do so when I'm engaged in a Rescue—I have done so, in fact—but it's not a function for which I am specifically paid, or wish to be paid."

He swished his hand in the water rushing by. "I think I understand."

"Do you?"

"Your first purpose is to help. That's how you see yourself. That's clear from your site. It's not the money; I noticed you've worked for free on more than a few occasions." He smiled, and shook his head as if in wonder. "Guardian angel is so you: when no one else will answer the cry for help, you will. I find that very . . ."

He seemed on the verge of an intimate revelation, one that—despite her self-imposed injunction against giddiness—she found herself eager to hear. Heart poised in anticipation, she met his eyes. "Yes?" she whispered.

His gaze locked with hers for a moment, then slid past her

shoulder. "We're coming up on the Spaceport," he said. "Better take her off auto."

***

The market was already set up, and thronged with customers. It occupied a space roughly the size of a soccer field, with two prominent displays of machinery and appliances where the goals would be. Even from a distance as they floated past, Yoelin could distinguish islands of stalls devoted to produce, food, herbs and spices, clothing, fabrics, small equipment, tools, and gee-gaws. There was even a booth for the purchase of "indents," according to the sign, which she took to mean indentured servants, and possibly slaves.

She felt her mouth draw down in a deep frown, and saw Stefan's expression change to one of concern.

"What is it?" he asked.

Words fumbled in her mind. In the glimpse of her past she could still hear the gavel bang, hear the barker announce a final bid of forty-three thalers. She could still see the leer on the buyer's face.

She shook her head so hard her eyes ached, and altered the kaleidoscope of her memories so that they had no meaning for her. "It's nothing," she said, and pointed to port. "We can tie up there. Fetch up the mooring rope, Stefan."

"Aye, Skipper."

As they sidled up to the slip pier, he leaped out and secured the rope to a cleat, then offered her a helping hand out of the boat. She took it, but dropped it as soon as she stood on the pier. For a moment she stood still, arms pressed against her flanks, feeling the side-arms under her loose jersey. Her hand went momentarily to a front pocket of her jeans, seeking the reassurance of the Palmetto. Even a skillful dip would have problems relieving her of any of the three items without her noticing. As long as she could feel the weapons against her skin, and the tightness of her jeans pocket, she was free to focus on spotting Manohra Dhu.

"How do you want to proceed?" asked Stefan.

She mulled over the possibilities. If Stefan were in fact in deep cover, her instructions to him were probably useless; worse, he would be able to base his actions on the knowledge of what she herself would be doing. But if he were as he presented himself to be . . .

She decided to play it straight, even though it meant listening to her heart and shunting aside her training. "You take the far half, and I'll take the near half," she instructed, as she surveyed the market. "You have a Palmetto and my code. If you spot her, ping me. Otherwise, take no action; just keep her in sight until I get to you." She turned to face him, and pushed a finger against his chest for emphasis and attention as she looked him in the eyes. "Stefan, everything about her suggests that she is a skilled security operative. Under no circumstances are you to close with her."

He smiled easily. "I'm not afraid—."

She shoved him. "You'd *better be* afraid. Damn it, Stefan, you're an *amateur.*" Passers-by drifted on the pier, and she lowered her voice to a conspiratorial whisper. "If Dhu thinks she's been made, there's no telling how she'll react. I don't want you to . . . to . . ."

"To get hurt?" he tried helpfully.

She looked away. Her lips moved, but she was unable at the moment to force any words out.

"Yoelin," he said, and she looked at him once more. "I will be careful, and I will not take any chances. I promise."

She hesitated, then nodded. "All right, then."

"As for what you're trying not to say to me," he went on. "I believe I'm trying not to say the same things to you—but having less success, as I'm the one who's just now brought it up."

Breath left her.

Ye gods.

She threw her gaze to the boat, the pier, the crowd, anywhere but at him. Finally she said, "Just remember, you're here to shop. That's your cover, your behavior pattern."

"Exactly. Which reminds me, I need a couple more brushes, and a tube of Venetian red."

She chuckled and shook her head, and walked off, blending with the crowd.

***

The stale sweat of some in the crowd blended with the vast array of other smells and seemed to form a haze that shimmered above the market. Until she merged with the crowd, Yoelin had not fully grasped the size of it. Accustomed to elbow room, she felt more than a little claustrophobic. Within seconds she was fighting the urge to break away, to find some fresh air and open space. Instead, she stood still and took a few moments to steel herself to the task at hand. Somewhere in this mass of people, many of them women with short dark hair, she expected to find her quarry . . . somehow. Soon she began to meander past stalls and alcoves, paying scant attention to the calls from barkers. Now and then she was jostled, and each time she immediately verified that she still retained her weapons and the Palmetto. Anyone who wanted her pocket lint was welcome to it.

The islands of booths had been arranged with about four meters of passageway between them, or just enough to accommodate the flow of traffic and allow customers to browse the wares. Yoelin was forced to pause here and there while people conversed, oblivious to their surroundings. She used the opportunities to scan the crowd, as if looking for a companion while she fingered some fabric or caught a scent of perfume. At one table she purchased a pouch of dried fruit and nuts for Ellie. The pauses served additional duty: she also checked for people keeping *her* under surveillance. She drew speculative appraisals from a couple of men, neither of whom made any effort to approach her or engage her in conversation. But no one else seemed interested in her one way or the other.

Though she found no sign of Manohra Dhu or of the dead man's associates, if any, Yoelin felt tension mount within her. The discovery of the existence of the market had planted a seed of possibility that had quickly grown into a certainty: Dhu was sure to show up here. Yoelin was unable to dismiss that certainty as delusional. If the woman was on Havelox Rest, she would attend the market on this day. The hologram promised as much.

So where the hell was she?

Yoelin paused at a booth of baked goods to think, keeping her senses open to her surroundings. With her back to the booth, the only threat from behind came from an old woman who wrapped the bread and pastries for sale. Even so, Yoelin kept her in the periphery while she dredged the market hologram from memory. What had particularly interested Dhu? She had been standing before a rack of bins, each of the contents a different color . . . a stall hawking grains and herbs and spices. Perhaps this revealed a culinary interest; Dhu liked to prepare meals from scratch. There had been nothing in the other documents to corroborate this interest, but perhaps those who had assembled the information did not deem it important enough.

Typical, she thought, mentally clucking her disapproval.

She raised up on her toes to look around, seeking out food stalls with similar bins. Right away she located two in an island three rows over . . . and Stefan already was watching one of them, or at least looking in its general direction. Moments later, he turned and walked away, heading for an island of miscellaneous stalls. Yoelin returned her attention to the island he had been watching, and soon spotted a woman wearing a billed cap over short black hair. She was standing at a stall of bins, her back to Yoelin, making little gestures with her hands that suggested she was haggling with the dealer. She was wearing a light blue camisole that set off the golden skin of her bare arms and shoulders, and blue jeans.

Yoelin moved off in her direction, taking care to use clusters of people as cover for her approach. She told herself the woman did not have to be Dhu, but she was surely worth checking out. So why hadn't Stefan pinged, so she could go check her out? Even as Yoelin drew closer, her heart felt leaden with disappointment. What Stefan had done amounted to a betrayal. Her heart tried to point out that he simply might not have noticed the woman, but her mind wasn't in a mood to listen. She had to focus on her job.

She reached the island and began to edge along the stalls, drawing closer to the woman. From this angle she could just make out a few features that suggested Asian ancestry. Her right hand went to her hip, feeling the Kreisler Energo lodged there under the jersey. Her mind willed the woman to turn her way, so that she could be certain. She reached the bins and paused, pretending to examine the contents. Each bin was covered by a clear lid, but had a little box for customers to sample freshness and texture. Absently her eyes took in various grains, including a wild rice she had never seen before, and herbs and colorful spices and seasonings. She drifted to within three paces of the woman, who was still talking with the dealer, and picked tentatively at a sample box of fresh basil.

As if abruptly aware of Yoelin, the woman turned to her and flashed a smile of impersonal courtesy. Yoelin had no choice but to return it. In that moment she knew she had found Manohra Dhu.

Dhu's right arm snaked out, her hand fluttering. "You have a . . . a thing on your shoulder," she told Yoelin. "It looks like a tiny red light."

Yoelin dove sideways toward Dhu, knocking her down in the collision. A scant second later one of the bins burst open, showering them with flakes of rolled oats.

012

Yoelin heard the faint report of the rifle a split second later. Sharp cries of alarm rained all around her like the grain, and people stumbled as they stepped back, as if uncertain what had just happened. Dhu wound up on her back. The metal of the automatic pistol ground into Yoelin's hip as she lay on her left side next to Dhu. The golden-skinned woman wore an expression of utter bewilderment. If it was an act, Yoelin decided, it was damned good.

She knew instinctively that lying on the ground surrounded by standing people kept her and Dhu out of the line and angle of fire. It also left them vulnerable to trampling if the crowd should panic. She suspected the shooter might escape in the excitement, but she could not count on that. For now, she had to assume he was still in the vicinity. She had to move—fast, and in unexpected ways to spoil his aim. Runchal's sons and other security personnel constituted another reason for her to leave the area, for inevitably they would arrive at the scene, and she was in no mood to talk to them just yet.

She made a flash decision, based on the fear and confusion in Dhu's golden eyes. She put her lips close to Dhu's ear. "Trust me for half an hour," she whispered. "No questions. I'll get you out of here."

Tiny furrows appeared on the bridge of Dhu's snub nose.

"Yes or no," pressed Yoelin. "We don't have much time."

Dhu gave a tight nod, and Yoelin relaxed slightly. The first obstacle had been hurdled. After scrambling to her feet, she helped Dhu up, and began tugging her along, their feet crunching on scattered grain and bin fragments. The dealer called after them, but Yoelin ignored him. The crowd parted slightly to allow them to pass, not sure what had just transpired but unwilling to involve itself. Yoelin headed for the boat in an irregular pattern. Two men rushed toward her, one dressed in red-on-white security livery, and for a moment she held her breath. But they passed by, barely brushing her shoulder.

"What—?" began Dhu.

"No questions," Yoelin repeated. "*Please* trust me."

Suddenly Stefan was standing ahead of them, in their path. His raised hand held an object Yoelin did not quite recognize. As they drew within a few steps, he said, "I found some cobalt blue, too. I can paint the highlights in your hair—."

Drawing abreast of him, she shot four knuckles into his solar plexus, then shoved him into a stall. "You didn't tell me you saw her," she yelled at him. As he spilled backward, struggling to breathe, she headed off at a trot, yanking Dhu along behind her. Wood squeaked, and she guessed that the stall frame had collapsed under Stefan's weight. She did not look back.

"That man," gasped Dhu.

"I couldn't allow him to stop us," she hissed, and pointed as they drew near the piers. "There, over there. Climb aboard, I'll cast off."

Across the inlet she spotted the Port Authority douane office. Already she had calculated angles, and had concluded that the shooter had probably lain on the roof of the office to take his shot. From that vantage point he would have had a good view through a telescopic lens down into the crowd, and been far enough away to avoid immediate notice after firing the shot. He was not there now. And she had not decided who he had meant to kill.

"At least tell me *something*," pleaded Dhu. Seated facing aft on the middle bench, she was perspiring now with the effort of their escape, and the top of her camisole was dark and wet. The thin fabric clung to her here and there. Her short black hair, also damp, was littered with flakes of grain.

Around them, others were departing from the market in their boats. Yoelin started the motor and eased the *Betha* out into the inlet, where they merged with a small fleet of boats heading toward the open sea. A white security boat twice their size cut around the fleet, heading for the pier.

Yoelin sat down on the stern bench. Her lips puffed out with a mighty burst of relief. For a few moments she regarded Dhu, facing her. A rash of emotions plagued Dhu's face, making a lie of stereotypical inscrutability. A notion crossed Yoelin's mind that she had just behaved most unprofessionally and might well have placed herself in jeopardy. She gave the notion a moment, then swatted it away. Earlier that morning she had sensed that something was awry with her contract. The event at the market, as far as she was concerned, removed all doubt from that vague assessment.

They reached open water, where the fleet scattered, each boat to its own destination. Yoelin looked around, and saw no large white boats in pursuit. She might catch hell later, when Runchal's people figured out what had happened, but for now she had a free hand. And less than half an hour, now, if she kept her word.

Dhu's tremulous voice was just audible. "Where are we going?" she asked. "What's going on?"

Yoelin turned the helm ten points to starboard, following several other boats along the west coast of Birdfoot Island. "Your name is Manohra Dhu," she said.

Golden eyes narrowed. "Do I know you?"

"No."

"But you know me."

Yoelin shrugged, and edged the *Betha* closer to shore, where a spit of land caressed a lagoon, affording visitors a measure of seclusion.

"Who are you?" asked Dhu, her voice strident now as fear crept into it.

"Until a while ago you worked as an office clerk in Corporatia Records on Jalune," said Yoelin.

Dhu was aghast. Hands fluttering, she lodged a protest. "I what? No, no, no. I've lived here all my life. I've never even *been* to Corporatia, and I never *will*." She tried to get to her feet, lost her balance as the boat shifted, and sat back down hard. "What's going on? Who are you? You said to trust you, and I-I *believed* you." Her pointed chin jutted. "You take me back right this instant."

Yoelin cut the engine and let the boat drift into the lagoon, her thinking accelerated. Dhu's statement, and the tone of voice in which she delivered it, compelled Yoelin to believe her. Exactly who this woman was remained a mystery, but she was certain this was not the Dhu she had contracted to find.

And there was something about the shooting itself . . . Yoelin could not quite touch her finger to it. She had been facing the rack of bins, and standing further from them than Dhu. Dhu had turned toward her, at an angle that enabled her to see the dot of the targeting laser . . . which meant that it might have simply grazed her on the way to aim at Dhu, and that her shoulder had merely interrupted the beam. The shattered grain bin had been in front of Dhu, just to her left. So which of them was the shooter firing at?

More questions surfaced. With no immediate answers, Yoelin had no choice but to dismiss them and focus on the present moment. "My name is Yoelin Thibbony," she said quietly, folding her hands in her lap in support of the appearance of harmless earnestness she was trying to create. "I was hired by Corporatia Security to come to Havelox Rest and find Manorha Dhu. You are, and look like, the person I was hired to find. But unless I am grossly mistaken, you are not the Manohra Dhu I was told I would find."

"That makes no sense at all."

Yoelin grinned, and nodded. "Exactly!" She prised the Palmetto from her pocket and had Abnoba call up the hologram of Dhu at the market. "This is you," she said. "In fact, I can now see that this was recorded at the Spaceport market."

Dhu nodded. "Three markets ago. But how—."

"You misunderstand, Manohra. I didn't record this. This hologram was *sent* to me as part of your dossier."

Her eyes widened. "I have a dossier?"

"So it seems."

"How can I possibly have a dossier? I'm of no interest to anyone. I just study marine life. And . . . it's Morning."

Yoelin glanced east at Karsh, its orange light filtering through the foliage at the tops of the island trees. "Yes, I know."

"No, I mean I'm called Morning," explained Dhu, calmer now. "Manohra is formal, and I never use it. It's the name of a wood nymph."

"You say you've been here all your . . . ," began Yoelin, and stopped as she spotted the dark shape in the water, approaching the boat from the starboard side. Abruptly she got to her feet and moved to a spot between Dhu and the water, arriving just as Ellie's head and neck appeared. Dhu's eyes widened. Yoelin said, "*No*, Ellie. *Friend*," punctuating it with what she hoped was a thought-image to that effect.

To Yoelin's astonishment, Dhu laughed, and said, "I don't believe it."

Mouth open, Ellie poised expectantly. Yoelin fished out the pouch of dried fruit and fed a piece to her by hand.

"It seems you have a friend," said Dhu.

"You sound surprised."

"I'm more surprised that I have a dossier," said Dhu. "I take it the two of you have bonded."

Yoelin fed Ellie another piece. "Bonded?"

"A young crippy can pick someone, much like a baby duck imprints the first living thing it sees," Dhu explained. "I don't know what the catalyst is; it seems to be random."

"Like a random act of kindness?" asked Yoelin.

"What did you do?"

"I just said hello to her."

Dhu nodded. "Sometimes that's all it takes. For any species."

"You said crippy."

"Yes, short for Cryptoclidus. Aquatic Terran dinosaur. The crippies fill that particular niche here; analogs, of course. They prune the algae and seaweed in the shallows."

Yoelin smiled. "Are those analogs, too?"

"Algae is a very simple life form," said Dhu. "Common to most oceans anywhere, and most species can live in oceans almost anywhere. What I was going to add was crippies aren't aggressive, but they can be very protective of the person they've bonded to."

"So they might kill someone," she said.

Dhu's answer was slow in coming. "Under the right circumstances, yes." Her golden eyes narrowed. "You sound as if—."

A splash of water cut her off, as Ellie slapped her neck against the surface of the ocean, and followed this with a bark.

Dhu scowled at the crippy, and plucked at her sodden camisole. "They do that for attention," she said ruefully. Her eyes narrowed. "Has Ellie killed someone?"

"She thought she was protecting me," said Yoelin, as she tossed out a couple pieces of pineapple.

"That explains your reaction when she showed up here. But the way you said 'friend' suggests you've had to call her off before."

"There are some people I wouldn't like to see hurt."

"Hopefully I'm one of them."

"Ellie knows you're a friend," Yoelin assured her.

"Good to know . . . wait, *how* does she know? Just because you say the word to her doesn't mean . . ."

"I don't think she understands words, so much as she does the thought behind them."

Dhu sighed, and nodded to herself. "So you know about that, too. *Damn.*"

Yoelin cocked an eyebrow at her. Gone was the problem of the market shooting, replaced by a puzzled curiosity. "Know that she's telepathic?" she asked.

Dhu clasped her hands between her knees and leaned forward, looked down at her feet on the deck. "Damn, damn, damn," she seethed. When she looked up, her eyes were wet. "We can't let that secret get out," she whispered. "And if someone like you knows, then someone in Corporatia knows."

"Someone like me?"

"A hired killer," Dhu said bitterly.

Stunned, Yoelin could only gape at her for a few moments. "I'm not," she said, "not a . . . the rifle was probably aimed at *me*, Morning."

"Then I don't understand."

"But why would someone want *you* killed?" Yoelin asked.

Dhu's expression reflected the disgust in her tone. "Because I've done the most research on the crippies," she replied. "I don't dare publish, of course."

Yoelin shook her head. "That's a good reason for keeping you alive."

As if to agree, Ellie barked, and splashed them.

"We have to find a secure place," said Yoelin. Her hand moved to restart the motor, but Dhu reached out to arrest her arm.

"There's no such place on Rest," Dhu said, and glanced up. "Even now they're looking for us on SECSAT. They have the whole planet covered. It's just a question of reaction time once they locate us." Abruptly she raised a hand for silence. "Listen," she whispered.

Yoelin heard it, too: a boat motor.

Ellie slipped beneath the surface of the water and began swimming toward the mouth of the cove. Unable to call out to her now, Yoelin thought hard, conjuring a negative image, telling Ellie no in an effort to get her to return, or at least to avoid danger. The motor grew louder, and presently the boat itself appeared, rounding to the mouth of the cove.

Stefan Coppenrath was kneeling on the deck in front of the aft bench under a makeshift white awning, hand on the helm, bearing the craft directly for them. Alongside, her head and neck a meter or so out of the water, swam Ellie.

A sense of rescue and security washed through Yoelin. Dhu gasped, as if she had felt it as well. Nevertheless, Yoelin drew her Kreisler and kept it trained on Stefan, who cut the motor and let the boat drift toward shore and the shelter of a clutch of overhanging trees several meters away from them. He seemed oblivious of the weapon in Yoelin's hand. When his boat stopped, he beckoned to her urgently to join him there.

Ellie paused beside the *Betha* and gave a little bark. Then she poised with her mouth open.

The sensation Yoelin now received was *friend*. She stared at Ellie for a moment, and shifted her attention to Stefan, who stood on shore now, waiting.

Gradually she lowered the Kreisler, and put it away.

Ye, she thought, *gods*.

013

They gathered on the shore, just beyond the crescent of sand that served as a beach. With regard to Stefan, Yoelin was fighting back two urges: to hug him, and to apply the Kreisler laser to burning her initials in various sensitive portions of his anatomy. As if aware of her inner conflict, Stefan was rubbing his chest and wincing. Dhu stood slightly to one side, eyeing Ellie warily as the crippy, at the edge of the water, waited with mouth open in anticipation.

Stefan broke the silence. "So she's what all the fuss is about," he said.

"You were looking right at her at the market," snapped Yoelin.

His eyebrows rose. "I was? When? Where?"

Yoelin swore softly. Accusation raised her voice half an octave. "She was standing right there at the grain bins, not five meters from you."

He studied Dhu as if trying to remember her, and shook his head. "I was envisioning a painting of the market, with . . . you know, that girl."

"I think I've seen you," said Dhu, jabbing her finger in his direction. "Aren't you the man who sits in the tavern and broods? Every once in a while you tear a sheet of paper out of some notebook, ball it up, and throw it away?"

"That would be me."

Ellie barked. Yoelin tossed her a piece of fruit.

"They'll be looking for you two," Stefan went on. He glanced up. "This canopy will conceal our movements, although eventually they'll see that you landed here." He took a moment to survey Dhu. "Your hat will slow their identification of you," he decided. "They won't have had a clear view. But they'll figure it out. Yoelin, we can't go to your place, it's too risky. They don't know about me, so we'll go to the place I've rented. Stay under the trees."

Yoelin hesitated, uncertain. "I can remote the *Sequana* here. We can—."

"Can never come back if we do that," Stefan broke in. "And I'd like to be able to come back here."

"I wouldn't be able to protect my crippies," Dhu added, and shook her head emphatically. "We can't leave them."

"That's not in my contract," said Yoelin.

"To hell with your contract," Dhu yelled.

Stefan cleared his throat for attention. "We could stand here and discuss it until security arrives," he said.

"They'll trace your boat," Yoelin pointed out.

"It's not mine," said Stefan. "It was moored to the security pier. I kept my face down to stymie ident; besides, it's going to be a while before they start looking for their own boat."

Yoelin moved toward the water and tried to project images to Ellie, among them the caution that she should move out to sea and avoid attention. She sensed opposition from the crippy, followed by a gradual and dejected acquiescence as Ellie slipped back into the water, as if the creature was grousing, *oh very well.*

Returning to the others, Yoelin started to lead the way, but stopped when she remembered she was not supposed to be all that familiar with it, and motioned Stefan to take the lead.

"Who *are* you?" Dhu asked her, as they followed him at about ten paces.

"I'm a substitute player," Yoelin answered, stepping carefully over a fallen tree. "Whenever the team runs into a rough patch, I sometimes get into the game and call plays until things get set right again. Then I go back to the sidelines and smoke a cheroot."

"I read that novel," said Dhu. "By Cervantes, wasn't it?" She nodded toward Stefan. "So who's he, Sancho Panza? Not Dulcinea, surely."

"For someone who avoids Corporatia," said Yoelin, "you know a lot about the civilization."

Dhu held a branch for her. "If you call Corporatia civilized. So who is he?" she persisted.

Yoelin shrugged. "We only met yesterday," she said, continuing to hold back from Stefan, and speaking softly. "I'm not sure which side he's on. You'd do well to remember that."

"So you don't know how he looks at you when you're not looking at him?" said Dhu, astonished.

"What?"

"Never mind. It's none of my business." She paused for a moment, and added, "What did Ellie have to say?"

"I told her to go out to sea and stay away from people. Not in so many words, of course."

Stefan had reached the crest of a low hill. "Hey, let's go, you two," he called back. "We need to get under cover."

Soon they passed within twenty meters of the hut Yoelin had leased, and she got her bearings, which she kept to herself. In her mind a list of priorities took shape, foremost among them getting in touch with Exeter to find out exactly where he stood. It was possible that The Axe had been unaware of the unusual travails she would experience on this contract, but she recalled that this was just the sort of contrary operation he liked to arrange when she was working for him. In that regard, he was as unreliable as Stefan.

They passed the remainder of the journey in silence. With too many strings tugging at her, Yoelin's mind balked, and she cleared it of all thought save the necessity of placing each foot carefully on the uneven terrain, to avoid turning an ankle or springing a knee. Manohra Dhu, matching her step for step, became as a wisp of fog in Yoelin's consciousness. Training, detached and independent, enabled her to keep watch over the woman, alert to any movement, however slight, that might be interpreted as hostile. Yoelin continued to stay back from Stefan as well, a prudent isolation.

Finally they drew near the hut he had leased. The hut where she had spent the bleakest years of a dark childhood. The hut she had feared. Incredibly, no quicksand of fear engulfed her on this visit. The structure seemed far less imposing—a pile of wood and tiles and acetate windows, nothing more. She might enter it, or kick it down, if she wished. The once-bloodstained ground near the entrance now nourished marigolds and wild understory, and moss-like ground cover in the permanent shade of nearby trees. The arrival amazed her. What was different now?

I'm *different*, she thought. I was here earlier, and I came away unscathed. It's just a small building. Just a place. Even now I'm facing far greater dangers. This hut is *nothing*.

I've won. I don't know how, but I've won. It can't ever hurt me again.

Elation swept over her shoulders, relaxing her. Wearing a private smile, she entered as Stefan held the door for her. She had been in here before, at his behest. She stepped to the back window and gazed out—at what, she could not say. She was aware of the surrounding forest, just as she was aware that Stefan had begun to brew coffee and that Dhu had sat down at the little dining table, her face turned toward the sunlight that issued through the side window, thin nostrils flaring with each breath as she recovered from the arduousness of the journey. Yoelin was aware of the enclosing hut, but no murky fears entered her mind or made her heart stutter. She knew only the peace of easy respiration, the tranquility of cool air.

I'm free. Ye gods, I'm free.

Only under firm control was she able to resist the urge to pirouette. To pump her fist. To cry out. To weep for joy. She kept control—she *had to* keep control—of her reactions because it was her secret, *her* victory.

The victory of Yoelin Thibbony over herself.

Of Deirdre Hanratty, over the past.

Her childhood memories held the relevance of a soap bubble that she had somehow finally managed to *poik*. Ephemeral, irrelevant. Her past did not signify. It had led merely to the present moment, and the person she had become. Other than that, the past did not matter. It had never mattered. Only the ever-advancing moment of *now*, mattered. *Living and doing*, mattered. That realization astounded her, and yet calmed her heart. Presently she found herself wondering whether her failure to return to Havelox Rest had been based on the fear of her memories, or simply on the monotony of water, of the omnipresent and all-encompassing ocean. On this world there were no mountains stained purple by distance, or great lush plains abound with multitudes of life forms, some grazing, some preying, some just standing there. No, it was a world of ocean freckled here and there with archipelagoes. Perhaps she had failed to return in order to avoid being bored rigid. A room with the same forever view always palled. Perhaps that was why she had *pieds-a-terre*, but no roots.

"The coffee smells good," Stefan announced.

Not, Yoelin noted, "Are you okay?" or some other expression of concern, for she knew she had been standing at the window for long moments. He was speaking to her as if they had already completed the preliminaries of encounter—the greetings, and the inquiries into states of health—and were now about to embark upon a trip through whatever thoughts and questions entered their minds. He was accepting her presence in the hut as if she had been there for some time, or perhaps had not departed after a previous visit. He was acting as if he assumed she belonged there, as the trees belonged in the forest, as the islands belonged in the water. As if she had been born to sit for him, to pose for him.

Doubts and questions aside regarding his loyalties, she would pose for him. It was decided. Naked, if he wished.

"Nude," she amended, aloud, nodding to herself.

Stefan looked slightly aghast. "I beg your pardon?"

"I'd love a cup, Stefan," she said, sitting down across the table from Dhu.

He peered at her through a shaft of sunlight as he poured. "You look different," he said, setting the mug on the table before her. "Something in the eyes."

"Getting shot at will do that," she said.

"No, this is something else." He looked around the hut. "Who would have thought I'd need a third chair here," he muttered.

Yoelin took a tentative sip, and burned the tip of her tongue. "Ellie told me you were a friend," she said, to Stefan.

Dhu perked up. "She *told* you that?"

"Not in so many words. More like images."

"You sound as if you doubt her," said Stefan.

Yoelin sighed. Stefan's comment was spot-on, and returned her to her conflict regarding him. She *did* doubt Ellie; she imagined the crippy had been fooled by some part of Stefan's mind. Now she was able to put her finger on the fact that had been gnawing at her, very subtly, since the events at the market. Stefan was an artist; whatever else he was, that much was clear. He had an eye for detail, for very specific detail. In the drawing he had made of her, he had seen something about her that made her look dangerous, and he had captured that. He had guessed, accurately, that she concealed a knife in her boot. He saw things that the average person, the average observer, would not see.

So how had he not seen that the woman at the grain bins might be Manohra Dhu? Because he had been enthralled by the budding concept of a painting? Mentally she shook her head. No, no.

Stefan was moving back now, to lean against the wall, as far as he could get from her and still remain inside the hut. She wondered whether he had seen something in her face, a furrow of puzzlement on the bridge of her nose, or perhaps a minatory sharpness in her eyes.

Under the table, her hand crept toward the butt of the Kreisler.

014

Sands in Yoelin's hourglass emptied, and time for her stood still. Only the questions continued to pass in review, a parade of doubts marching to the distorted tune of her original assignment. Stefan Coppenrath warped her certainties. The sum total of the observations and remarks he had made during their brief acquaintance said he had to be more than an artist, yet even as just an artist he had failed to notice the one detail that was important to her. As a mole operative for Corporatia Security, he had to have spotted Manohra Dhu. Even as an artist, attentive to detail, he had to have spotted her. His excuse for not having done so—pausing for creative reflection—sounded lame, yet it was plausible, if he were only an artist.

Dhu posed questions of a different sort. Clearly a woman going by that name had an official dossier with Corporatia, yet the woman who was now sitting at Stefan's table claimed that was impossible. Take her denial at face value, Yoelin decided. What did that mean? Unknown to this Dhu, someone had been keeping an eye on her studies and research. Either that someone was local, reporting to an intelligence handler in Corporatia, or it was an operative dispatched by Corporatia to Havelox Rest specifically to watch Dhu. If the latter, it would mean that prior information had been sent to Corporatia to cause the dispatch of the operative.

In either case, then, someone local had to have been keeping an eye on Manohra. Stefan Coppenrath fit that possibility. He also fit the possibility of a mole.

He also fit the possibility of an ingenuous artist.

Yoelin emitted a low growl of vexation. The hourglass reversed now, time began to count once more. For the other two people in the hut, perhaps five seconds had passed. Stefan now stood with arms folded across his chest, still leaning back against the wall. Dhu had begun to sip her coffee.

Yoelin let her hand drift away from her sidearm. She drew a sharp breath and said, to Stefan, "Cobalt blue?"

He seemed to relax a little, despite his watchful gaze. "Your hair is so intensely black in the sunlight," he said. "The highlights are deep blue."

"I didn't realize."

"I might have captured them in ultramarine," he went on. "But cobalt blue is perfect for you."

"Stefan, . . ."

"After a year of training," he went on smoothly, "I served for almost two years with Special Operations, Corporatia Security."

Dhu gasped, and slowly turned to stare at him, eyes wide and incredulous. Yoelin's shoulders stiffened in preparation for quick and decisive action, although none seemed necessary at the moment, toward either individual. Stefan had made the revelation as he might have made a remark in an ongoing conversation about the weather. It's hot today, thunderstorms tomorrow, I spy on folks and sometimes kill them, should cool off in another day or so.

The abrupt and unexpected announcement tumbled Yoelin into a moment of stunned silence, even though she had halfway been expecting something of this nature. The muscles of her cheeks clenched, bulging at the corners of her jaw, while she resisted the urge to throttle him. Finally she prompted, grating, "And you tell me this now because?"

"*You've* been sending reports of my research," snapped Dhu, and started to rise from her chair.

"No, Morning," said Yoelin. "It's not him."

The golden woman whirled back to her. "How can you say that?" she cried. "You *heard* him—."

"Exactly," agreed Yoelin. "If he were the one, why would he reveal himself."

"Maybe that's how he *wants* you to think," Dhu returned.

"Yeah, perhaps. But the convolution of reasoning has to stop somewhere, Morning, and I'm going to stop it there. It's not Stefan."

"*Who*, then?"

"Stefan?" said Yoelin, and cocked an eyebrow expectantly.

"I don't know," he answered.

"All right. Why reveal your past now?"

"If it *is* his past," Dhu put in, grousing.

"Because I could sense where your thoughts were taking you," he said. "My training, remember? Just because I'm no longer active doesn't mean I no longer remember."

Yoelin's face twisted. "How many negatives is that?"

"The point is," sighed Stefan, "that you were on the verge of allowing me to become a misdirection. I'm trying to help you, Yoelin. I'm trying to get you to look elsewhere, not as a ruse to divert you from me, but because until you are convinced that the threat comes to you from outside, you won't look for it there, and I'm sure you know how dangerous that can be." He spread his hands in a plea for understanding. "As for what happened at the market, yes, I see what I did, or didn't do. I get it. I've been replaying it in my mind. Yes, I saw her," he made an airy gesture, "this woman. But I didn't see see her. I was seeing *you*, Yoelin. I was seeing that girl. I was . . . envisioning. My art is my safe haven. If we are to . . . okay, I can't say that, but you have to understand about my art. It's where I go whenever I catch even a glimpse of past events. Maybe you don't get that. Maybe there's nothing in your past that you need to balance with something positive in your present. But there is in mine." He paused, peering at her. "What's wrong?"

Yoelin slowly rose to her feet. The hard-won victory over her past and her fears remained intact, somewhat to her surprise. She realized she had just passed a test. Nevertheless, she felt a hollow in the pit of her stomach. "You have no idea," she whispered, hoarse because her mouth was dry. "You have no idea what happened in my past, or how I try to balance it in my present. *None.*"

"So you became a guardian angel."

Her scowl was a thundercloud. "You know too much, Stefan, damn you. Is that why you watch me when you think I'm not looking? So that you can know me bet . . ." She broke off and dashed to the front window, drawing up alongside it to peer around the jamb.

"What is it?" he asked, sudden concern shaking his voice.

"Not watching me," she said, her voice even and calm now, as if the wait for danger had ended, now that it was upon them, and she could combat it—if she could spot it. How much time did they have? "Not watching you, either, Stefan," she went on, thinking aloud.

"You and I are in it only by association." She shot a glance at Dhu. "Morning, it's *you* they're watching. There's an eye on you *all the time*. As long as no one interfered with you, they'd leave you alone. When Stefan and I showed up at the market, they panicked . . . ah. A security boat, out on the water." She pulled back from the window and withdrew the Palmetto. "You two, outside now. No questions. Move!"

Stefan, to her relief, ushered Dhu through the doorway. As soon as they were clear, she squeezed her eyes shut and thought hard, conjuring images.

Ellie. Tell your people to get to deeper waters and stay out of sight. Bad people coming to hurt you. To hurt us.

The imaged response shocked her. *We will protect you.*

I have to go, Ellie. I will come back.

. . . sadness.

Eyes moist, Yoelin rushed from the hut, keyed the Palmetto and said, "Abnoba, *home*."

Within a second, an indigo ellipsoid with green trim appeared on top of the hut, crushing it to splinters. Automatically, because the entire *Sequana* was in emergency status, the boarding ramp extruded. With Yoelin alternately shoving Dhu and Stefan ahead of her, they boarded the ship. As soon as the ramp retracted and the hatch sealed, the spaceskiff entered a pre-set Track into N-space and poised there, the computer awaiting further instructions.

"Runchal will never forgive this violation," said Stefan, as they made their way forward to the bridge.

Only then did Yoelin realize fully what she had done by having *Sequana* home in on her position. She pulled up short in the gangway, scarcely aware of the two bodies swerving around hers. The dark and dreadful hut of her childhood memories was no more. She had smashed it flat, like so much kindling. The last link between what had been then and what could be now, was broken. *Free*, she thought. *Free*.

There had been a relatively small price to pay for that last bit of freedom, and she had not paid it. "I'm sorry about your art and supplies," she said, to Stefan. "Truly I am. I'll replace what you need."

He dismissed this with a wave of his hand. "Except for the sketches I made of you, it was all very bad painting. I can do so much better, now. But I'd hoped to come back because of . . . the girl. Now," he sighed. "Now, I don't know."

"What are you two on about?" Dhu yelled as they reached the bridge. "What about my *crippies*?"

"You can't help them if you're *dead*," said Yoelin. "Stefan, you get the starboard chair. Morning, pull out that bench from the bulkhead and have a seat."

"Not until you tell me what the *fuck* is going on," Dhu screeched.

"I'm about to," she said. "Now sit down. Please."

Glaring at her, Dhu obeyed. Stefan followed her lead by seating himself.

"That shot at the market was meant for me," said Yoelin, more to Stefan than to Dhu. "In their panic, they chose to kill me to keep me from her. More precisely, to keep Exeter and Corporatia Security from getting her. It might have worked, had she not noticed the target laser on my shoulder. With that opportunity missed, they had to revert to their back-up plan, which was to eliminate her. They've had eyes on her constantly. It just took them a bit of time to mount an assault, by boat. I saw two on the water, heading toward the hut. They knew exactly where she had taken refuge, Stefan."

"You said 'they,'" Stefan pointed out.

Yoelin shrugged. "Whoever 'they' are." She leaned back in her chair. "There's just one more thing," she went on. "Abby, personal scan."

"Neither is carrying a tracer of any kind."

"Scan me as well, Abby."

"You do not have a tracer of any kind."

That stumped her. "What about the *Sequana* herself?"

"There is a camouflaged tracer affixed to the hull approximately zero point five two—."

"Abby!"

"Sorry. I forgot. About half a meter directly in front of the boarding hatch."

"You *forgot?* Abby, you're a computer. You don't forget . . . oh, never mind. I'll adjust your personality later. Abby, why didn't you tell me about this?"

"You did not ask."

"It's a *security* matter. You're supposed to report it *directly it occurs.* Ye *gods,* Abby." She heaved a heavy sigh. "Adjust, hell. I'll do a complete overhaul. All right, Abby, who emplaced the tracer?"

"Unknown."

"Okay. *When* was it emplaced?"

"Five days ago at approxi . . . just before midday."

Yoelin frowned at this, thinking hard. Retracing her steps, she realized she had been on Providence at about that time, making arrangements for a painting. *But that would mean—.*

"That sounds as though you expected some other response," Stefan broke in. "What, may I ask?"

Yoelin shook her head. "I had no expectations at all," she shot back, unwilling as yet to divulge her thinking. Irritation tried to set in, an unwanted distraction, and she swatted it away. "But overall I'd say they've had a directional microphone on you, Stefan, and probably on me as well. That's probably how they knew we'd be at the market." She punctuated this with a seething epithet that caused him to draw his head back a little.

"I don't understand any of this," Dhu whined.

Yoelin grimaced. "It looks like we're going from The Dragons to the Lion's Den," she said, to no one in particular. "Abby, calculate a course for Providence. Arrival orbit first, then the spacepad on Dannik Exeter's estate."

"Calculated."

"Wait," said Dhu. "What about that tracer?"

"Abby, scramble the tracer's stickum while we're in N-space," ordered Yoelin. "Let it slip free and float around in there forever."

"Acknowledged."

Stefan looked to Yoelin. "Is that wise, going to see Exeter?"

Yoelin grinned without mirth. "No. Punch it, Abby."

"Do what?"

She rolled her eyes. "Just enTrack us, Abby. Let's go."

015

Ensconced safely in N-space, the three repaired to the galley for coffee, to a litany of complaints from Dhu. "My research documents are as good as gone," she lamented. "I might be able to reconstitute some of them, over time. But by then the damage will have been done. Corporatia R&D will study what I did and contrive experiments for the crippies to find the optimal ways to weaponize their telepathic abilities." Her golden eyes narrowed as she sipped from her mug, both hands clasped around it as if to absorb the warmth from the liquid. "And what, exactly, are you planning to do with me?" she asked Yoelin.

"My contract calls for me to retrieve the documents you stole and turn them over to Corporatia Security," she replied. "Specifically, to Dannik Exeter."

Dhu was aghast. "But-but I didn't steal any documents."

"Well, that does present a problem, doesn't it?"

Stefan cleared his throat for attention. "Maybe what Exeter wants is the documentation regarding the crippies," he suggested.

Yoelin nodded. "I've been thinking along those same lines. I grab her, grab the documents in her possession and those at her residence, under the assumption that they are the relevant ones, and turn her over to him, and get paid."

"Or silenced," said Stefan.

"Yes. Or silenced." She shut her eyes for a moment, breathing softly, her chest barely moving under the dark blue jersey as she reviewed the conflicting information and possibilities. Earlier she had assembled a cogent interpretation of the facts regarding the attack at the market. Now, upon reflection, she had doubts. If the attack was not meant to kill her or Dhu, but instead to goad her into precipitate action . . . but to what possible end?

"Why guardian angel?" Dhu piped up.

Yoelin opened her eyes, and blinked. "What?"

"That's what he called you," Dhu went on. "Something about

your past."

Unwilling to discuss it with her, Yoelin waved her off. "It's not important."

"Because I certainly could use a guardian angel about now," said Dhu, as if there had been no dismissal. "I'm being set up. I have no idea why. You said I wasn't the Manohra Dhu you had been sent to find. I had no idea there was another me, anywhere." She paused, and drew a steadying breath. "So how do I go about hiring a guardian angel?"

"Get in line," Yoelin replied, unsure whether she would regret the rejection. Only her own rules applied, after all; she might readily accept, if she wished. At the moment, however, she did not wish. "I'm already on contract. After that, Stefan has engaged me to find someone for him."

A touch of fear entered Dhu's voice. "You're not for hire?"

"Not right now."

"Don't turn me over to anyone," pleaded Dhu. "Just take me back to Rest. Let me do my work."

"It's a challenge," Stefan put in. "Your contract trying to hire you for a contract."

Yoelin glowered at him. "Don't *you* start."

"What if she's not your contract?" he asked.

"How do you mean?"

"If she's not the Manohra Dhu you were engaged to locate," he explained patiently, "then she's not your contract. If you're willing, she can engage you."

"But we don't *know*—."

Stefan held up a hand. "A trifle."

Dhu set her empty mug on the counter and sighed. "I wish I knew what was going on."

"I'm not sure I do," Yoelin said slowly. "Exeter just follows orders. If he's ordered to hire an independent operator such as myself, someone outside the system at present, he would do so. Or he might do so on his own, not wanting to risk assigning one of his own people. I can't speak to his motivations in that regard. But the point here is that," she paused to refill her mug, "is that Exeter may not have been given all the information. In fact, the more I think about it, the more I suspect that's likely. I think someone has been playing a long game here. This isn't about Corporatia R&D weaponizing the crippies. Someone else, some other organization, aims to do that."

"But why?" asked Stefan.

She gave him a wry smirk, as if he should know. "Well, why?"

His voice hushed. "You-you're talking about a coup."

Yoelin slowly nodded, and looked at Dhu. "It depends on the capabilities of the crippies," she said. "Whether they can be used, and whether they can in fact do what that organization wants them to do."

Dhu thrust her hands into the pockets of her jeans, as if she wanted no part of the questions or the possibilities. As she turned away, Yoelin caught her by the shoulder and gently but firmly twisted her back around.

"*Can* the crippies be used?" Yoelin pressed.

Dhu refused to meet her eyes. "I-I don't know. I'm not sure."

"There's another question," Stefan said quietly, in a tone that compelled Yoelin to look at him. "If I understand your plan correctly, you mean to turn this woman over to Dannik Exeter, claim your pay, and be on your way. The purpose of surrendering her to Exeter is to keep your putative covert organization from getting her and her work."

"That's the basic idea," Yoelin agreed.

"But you *can't*," breathed Dhu.

"What if Exeter is a part of that organization?" Stefan went on. "What if your contract is part of a ploy to acquire her?" He glanced at Dhu and added, "Acquire you."

Yoelin shook her head. The counter-arguments queued up. She watched them rise and take their places, and she looked to the first one, arming herself.

Before she could speak, he continued. "As Director of Corporatia Security he is in an ideal position to support a coup, or even to acquire autocratic power himself. Even if he is not part of this, they would try to find a way to use him, simply because of the information he controls."

"I've thought of this," Yoelin shot back. "Don't you think I've considered that possibility? And I'm telling you that is not Dannik Exeter. As Director he's a bastard. In his personal life he is occasionally unsavory, in ways I would prefer not to know about. But he does his job; he is dedicated to it." She whirled away, and made for the bridge. "It's not him," she threw over her shoulder.

"And if it is?" Stefan called.

"Then we're all dead."

She reached the bridge, heart pounding. Arms braced on the instrumentation console, she leaned forward, breathing deeply. In the back of her mind she knew Stefan was right to question Exeter's role. But he had obviously mulled over the possibility to a far greater extent than her own cursory examination and dismissal of it. She had worked for Exeter for better than five years, the last three directly for him, receiving her briefings and orders in his office. She could gauge his expressions and his nuances, even to the twitch of his left nostril that indicated he was being less than truthful. It could not be him.

Could it?

He was not above abandoning one of his operatives to the wolves, if that meant the success of the operation. Aside from that, he backed his people; in some cases she knew of, more than he should have done. On too many occasions when she had bucked other authority, he had backed her.

It could not be him.

"*Damn* it, Axe," she seethed, and struck the console with her fist.

She felt Stefan and Dhu return to the bridge. She did not turn around, but instead stared at the Videx blanked now by N-space. She saw her reflection there, and the reflections of her companions, and considered the word. *Companions.* It could not apply to Dhu, who was no more and no less the subject of the Rescue she had agreed to perform. Yet there was something vulnerable about the golden woman. She was out of her depth and she knew it, and she did not know what to do about it, but instead of worrying about herself, she was focused on what would happen to her self-assigned charges, the crippies. If anyone merited a guardian angel, it was Manohra Dhu, called Morning.

Companion could apply to Stefan. Despite the conflict he had presented her, she accepted Ellie's evaluation of him. Whatever else he might be, he was a friend. But what else was he?

She turned around to face them. Words formed in her mind, but Abnoba's one-word announcement blotted them out.

"Providence."

***

The stricken expression on Stefan's face told Yoelin to expect adversity when she returned her eyes to the Videx. Even so, she hoped it would not prove as bad as all that.

At first glance, it did not. A swatch of the northern half of Providence's largest continent hung like a diorama in the Videx, Abnoba zooming in on a thousand-kilometer-long rectangle centered around Exeter's estate, though the actual distance of the *Sequana* from the planet was the standard ten thousand kilometers. From west to east the expanse included a segment of a north-south cordillera, a vast plains drained by a system of meandering rivers, and a stretch of forested rolling terrain around the estate. The mansion itself, a sprawling edifice of quarried stone and brick framed by oak, whose wings were erected at different times, glistened in the morning light of the yellow dwarf known as Rhodile. Dannik Exeter had chosen a place of idyllic tranquility in which to contemplate his extensive and private collection of classic art. The estate was quiet.

Too quiet, thought Yoelin. She peered closer, and spotted the plume of blue smoke that issued from the peak of the east wing gable. Stefan must have noticed it immediately; it irked her that she had not done so first. For just a moment her heart formed a stone in her throat. Then she swallowed, and studied the mansion with as much detachment as she could muster.

The art collection did not concern her, secure and sealed as it was in its reinforced concrete bastion half a kilometer below the surface of Providence. The mansion, however, was guarded—was supposed to be guarded—by a small detachment of troops as well as by electromagnetic surveillance. A defensive perimeter should have been established, and fire-fighting equipment put into use. Yet nowhere did she see any sign of human life.

"Zoom in further," said Stefan, now standing beside her, his quiet voice insistent.

Yoelin issued the instruction. Stefan's right arm shot out, his index finger aimed. "There," he said.

Two uniformed bodies lay on the ground, partially hidden by a bank of lilacs. Yoelin saw one leg bent at the knee at an unnatural angle, and bit at her lower lip, sympathizing. With the magnification, other bodies quickly resolved themselves into view. She counted eleven, and stopped counting. All were in uniform; none, as far as she could tell, was Dannik Exeter.

"Abby, raise Exeter," she said, her voice taut with fear.

At first they heard silence, without even a background hiss to suggest that communications had been opened. To Yoelin, it was as if the link at the other end did not exist. She half-expected to hear a computerized voice break in to render an apology and announce that the code she had tried to link to was no longer in service. Instead, Dannik Exeter's voice broke through, crusty and fuzzy, as if the connection were ever-so-slightly misaligned.

"It's good to hear you, Yoelin," he said, pronouncing her name correctly. He did not offer to go to visual communications. "Let's forego sharing our locations for the moment. I gather your travels have gone well?"

"I even bought you a souvenir, sir," said Yoelin, to a gasp from Dhu. A violent chop of her hand shushed the protesting woman. "Where would you like me to put it?" she asked.

She could almost feel Exeter thinking. Finally he said, "I'm sure you recall your Dante."

Yoelin grinned crookedly. "Indeed I do. Half an hour?"

"About that," said Exeter, and closed commo.

Stefan cocked an eyebrow at her. "Dante?" he asked. "That doesn't narrow it down much."

Sprawled in the captain's chair, Yoelin stretched her arms and legs, relieved of a great worry. "You're right," she agreed, stifling a yawn. "There is much in *The Divine Comedy* that is worth quoting. But if you're familiar with it, you shouldn't even have to look up this one."

Dhu cleared her throat. "'*Lasciate ogni speranza, voi ch'entrate*,'" she intoned.

Startled, Yoelin gaped at her. "I thought you renounced Corporatia and all its works and pomps."

"'All hope abandon, ye who enter here,'" mused Stefan. "So, we're going through the Gates of Hell?"

Yoelin laughed softly. "Um . . . no. Quite the opposite, I should think, Stefan, as far as you're concerned. It's a private jest between The Axe and me, in reference to an assignment he gave me when I first started out. Where we're going, one word in the quotation is altered."

"I can't wait to see this," Dhu said drily.

"I'll remember you said that," Yoelin told her, smothering more mirth. "Abby, calculate a course for Ouvert, and take—."

"Calculated."

Yoelin sighed. "Yes, thank you, Abby. Now take us to Ouvert, there's a good computer."

016

Yoelin almost ran into Manohra Dhu as the shorter woman braked to a halt at the bottom of the *Sequana*'s extruded ramp. Yoelin gave her a little nudge. "Keep going," she urged.

Dhu refused to budge. "But this is a *nudist* colony!"

"So it is," chuckled Stefan, behind them.

Yoelin pointed at the inscription on the metal archway, through which they had to pass. "It's a nudist *planet*," Yoelin said, as she began to shepherd them toward the Visitors' Acclimation Compound. From her right hand dangled a green canvas belt with an open holster attached, bearing her Kreisler Energo. "'All clothing abandon, ye who enter here.' That's why Exeter chose this location. Only under very special circumstances can anyone bear arms, and even then you have to carry them openly." She made a little gesture of encouragement. "Come on, we can check our clothing at the VAC."

Dhu remained utterly aghast as she stared at the people on the other side of the archway, where the rest of Ouvert awaited them under swirling rose-colored clouds. "You cannot be serious," she said primly.

Yoelin indicated a trio of rather sturdy women standing to one side of the compound. "They'll assist you in undressing, if necessary," she said. "With a very few temporary exceptions necessitated by certain professions, nudity is the law here."

Dhu started to turn back around. "I'll just stay on board."

"That's not an option for you, Morning."

"*Damn* you."

"If you're concerned about assault," Yoelin went on, "that simply does not occur here." She grinned, and added, "Although I understand there is some consensual activity, now and then, here and there."

"It's not *funny*."

Yoelin sighed. "Okay, Morning, you've made your point. That's enough. We're here, so start peeling down. There are plastic bags provided for your clothing. Just hand yours to that clerk, and memorize the number he gives you. It'll be D-something, assuming you give him your right name."

"But . . ."

Yoelin and Stefan, already barefoot, stripped off their jerseys and began to divest themselves of their jeans. After a few more seconds of hesitation Dhu, still muttering, addressed her blue camisole with exaggerated deliberation, then her blue jeans.

Naked now, Yoelin looked Stefan over, as he did her. Succumbing momentarily to her prurient side, she noted that, like his shoulders, the rest of him looked fit enough. He, however, seemed to be regarding her with different eyes. They swept over her body again and again as if to absorb every nuance of her angles and curves for capture later in oil on canvas, or in graphite and charcoal on paper. As if to assess the effects of light and shadows on her skin, in the way she stood, one leg slightly akimbo, arms folded loosely across her chest without obstructing his view. She gazed at him with one eyebrow raised, inviting comment.

"I imagine there are a lot of suitable models on Ouvert," he said, his tone low and serious. "But now, even more than before, I want just the one, Yoelin. I want you."

Yoelin felt her face warm as she shifted her attention back to Dhu. Now that the camisole had been removed, the relative evenness of color on the skin of Dhu's upper torso suggested that she had spent a considerable amount of time in sunlight without a top.

And without a bottom, Yoelin added mentally, as Dhu completed her task and stood with her right arm and left hand firmly in place for as much modesty as she could summon under the circumstances. For a second or two Yoelin felt pity for the woman, whose evident lack of body consciousness while among the crippies did not carry over to human company. "I am sorry about this," Yoelin said gently. "But it's a necessary step if we are to try to resolve whatever is going on around us. Morning, we're all in danger now."

"But you're going to turn me over to him," Dhu sniffed. "Some resolution."

"Truthfully, I don't think Exeter wants you," soothed Yoelin.

"He wants someone else."

"I . . . hope so." Dhu gazed out at the other side of the archway once again, and sighed, still trying to cover herself. "At least he isn't ogling me, us," she added, with a glance at Stefan.

"I'm an artist," Stefan said sagely. "I don't ogle. I consider and contemplate."

"Speak for yourself," said Yoelin, strapping the green canvas belt around her waist. "And Morning, you're going to draw attention to us if you don't relax. Just walk around as if you still have clothes on. I doubt you or any of us will be ogled—it's socially gauche here—but if it happens . . . hell, I don't know. Ogle back, or ignore it."

"But . . . oh, all right." Dhu slowly lowered her hands to her sides. "Why do you get to wear something, and we don't?"

"I'm here on official security business," Yoelin explained. She slipped a red plastic card from a slot on the outside of the holster and held it up to them for display, then showed it to the trio of women, one of whom finally nodded. "Exeter and I, and about a dozen others in Corporatia, are holders of red security cards. This means, among other things, that I'm allowed to go armed on Ouvert. But not clothed."

"I hope you'll pose for me like that, too," said Stefan.

Yoelin frowned at him. "Why?"

"Why? Yoelin, have you any idea how erotic you look?"

The question struck her like a blow from an unexpected direction. On other occasions she had considered her attire in terms of allurement, but not at this particular moment. She was wearing, after all, a common web belt of rough-textured canvas, and a sidearm. What was erotic about that? But if Stefan was regarding her from that perspective, how would others on Ouvert see her? For a moment or two she debated whether to meet with Exeter unarmed, if for no better reason than to reduce the attention others might pay her. But Exeter himself might be armed, and his allegiance in this present contract remained in doubt. Moreover, he might have minions in the area who were armed. She could ill afford to go around defenseless.

"You'll just have to get over it, Stefan," she told him, quietly but firmly. "This is no time for fantasies."

He looked away. "I know that," he said. "It's just that . . . Yoelin, you've become my Muse."

"Oh, ye gods, Stefan."

"Can we just get this over with?" Dhu put in, dejectedly.

After they checked their clothing with the VAC clerk, Yoelin inquired after Exeter with Registration, not altogether disappointed to fail to find his name in the log. But how would he have registered? She frowned as she scrolled along the log, and twice passed over Benedetto Caetani before the name sank in. Chuckling lightly, she asked about him and learned that he had taken a bungalow with a patio about half a kilometer west of the spaceport. She let a small airfoil and got her charges boarded up, and they set out for Exeter. Although she received several curious looks which she assumed were connected with her sidearm, no one interfered with their progress. Nevertheless, she remained alert not only to the looks, but for any sign that they might be watched unduly. Ouvert was a relatively secure planet, but someone had attacked Exeter's estate, a tactic that entailed substantial risk. If the opposition, whoever it was, could undertake such an assault there, it certainly could do so on Ouvert.

The glideway took them parallel to the shore of a vast lake, and then into gently rolling terrain covered with grass and wildflowers. The possibility of attack clashed with the overall tranquility of the scenery, and Yoelin tried to shut the tension from her mind and yet remain alert. They came onto a meandering river that eventually straightened and plunged over some bluffs into a whitewater rapids, where a few kayakers attired only in life-vests tested themselves against the waters. Off to the right, glistening whitely in the overhead sunlight that pierced the pink clouds, a row of bungalows afforded lodging for visitors, and Yoelin banked the airfoil toward the third one from the end.

"I thought there would be more people," said Stefan.

Yoelin shook her head. "The permanent residents number maybe two million, planet-wide," she said. "Ouvert used to see a lot of curiosity-seekers and . . . other types, but they've learned how to discourage that. Most visitors nowadays come to see whether this particular lifestyle is for them. The majority of them soon discover that it is not. As a species, we're practically hard-wired to wear clothing. Ah, I see he's expecting us."

Stefan squinted. "Where?"

"On the patio at the side of the bungalow. He's positioned himself strategically at the table."

Dhu stood up and for a moment seemed to be contemplating whether to leap from the airfoil

"Stefan," Yoelin said quietly.

He grasped Dhu's wrist and tugged her back down to the stern bench. The air went out of her, and she slumped against the side of the airfoil, despondent. Yoelin nursed the airfoil onto a docking pad in front of the bungalow, and climbed down, the others following.

Exeter did not get up to greet them, but waved them to cushioned patio chairs at the table. He had, Yoelin noted, already acquired a mild sunburn, and his skin glistened with U-V block. Although she knew he would be armed, his weapon was not evident, and she wondered where he had cached it. His hard gray eyes regarded her thoughtfully while she waited for Stefan and Dhu to seat themselves before she took the last chair.

"You've added a couple scars, I see," Exeter said.

"And meted out a few others, Director," Yoelin returned.

"It seems you also remember your Dante."

"Who consigned Caetani, or Pope Boniface VIII, to the Eighth Circle of Hell."

"One circle above where you'd place me, I daresay."

Yoelin smiled without humor. "I daresay." A desultory wave of her hand indicated Dhu. "Here she is."

But Exeter had already turned his attention to Stefan. "You look familiar," he said.

"Eleven years ago I was with SpecOps," Stefan explained. "Maybe you saw me there. As for what I do now, I believe you own my *Young Girl in Sunlight.*"

It secretly pleased Yoelin to see a flash of astonishment on Exeter's face. He said, "You're Copper?"

Stefan inclined his head politely.

"What about me?" Dhu worried, fidgeting in her chair. "I want to know what's going to happen."

With obvious reluctance Exeter shifted to her. "You are Manohra Dhu." It was not a question.

Dhu sighed impatiently. "Yes," she hissed.

"And the archives she stole?" said Exeter, now addressing Yoelin. "Where are they?"

Yoelin's lips tightened. "You and I both know this woman had nothing to do with that, Director. Assuming, of course, that the archives even exist, and were in fact stolen. The fact that you are here, and not at your estate, is ample proof that, whatever is going on, it's not what you led me to believe. Now, I have fulfilled the terms of my contract to the extent that it is possible to fulfill it. I'll expect my Barcle's account to reflect a deposit of three million thalers within the next Standard day." She paused, and tilted her head at him. "Or would you rather I took my payment in art?"

"No, no," Exeter said quickly. "No, that's quite unnecessary. I'll have your account credited. Yoelin . . ."

She waited. Stefan opened his mouth as if to speak, and she hushed him with a hand to his knee, squeezing it.

Exeter licked his lips, and took a sip from a glass of ice water. "You saw what was done to my estate," he said. "The automatic fire extinguishing system should limit damage to the interior, but I'm afraid massive repairs are in order before the place becomes comfortably habitable again. After they killed the security staff, they searched the mansion, and killed the cleaning and kitchen staff."

"I'm sorry," said Yoelin. "Truly."

He averted his eyes briefly, his gaze distant. "Yes. Well," he said, his voice momentarily coarse. He cleared his throat and returned his attention to her. "I managed to get one of them alone and . . . ask him a few questions."

"I can imagine," Yoelin said grimly.

"Their orders were to capture me and take me to Cabarre."

"Out in The Dragons," she noted.

"Its reputation is growing as a hotbed of dissent," said Exeter. "Most folks who leave Corporatia are slackers and malcontents who simply don't want anything to do with it. With us. They live out there as best they can. But some of those who go to Cabarre have other plans. Rather grandiose plans, I might say. They talk a lot about changing Corporatia, but it's mostly talk, with a few activists now and then who think blowing up a child-care center is going to help their cause." He took another sip, emptying the glass. "We try to keep an eye and ear on matters out there, but we don't have enough personnel to spare to do a proper job, and in any event we're not really very welcome."

"I wonder why," Dhu muttered, without bothering to conceal the bitterness in her tone.

"But this is different," said Yoelin.

Exeter nodded. "This time they seem to have purpose and motivation, and apparently they think they have an unassailable weapons system. Before we go on, would any of you care for something to drink? Something stronger than, say, water? Danelle," he called, and a young woman with long yellow hair appeared at the side door of the bungalow. "I recommend gin and tonic," Exeter told them, "as that's all I managed to bring with me."

Only Dhu declined the offer of refreshments. She drew herself up in her chair with dignity and said, "I would like to know my status, if you please. Am I a prisoner? Am I free to go?"

"I think that's a fair question, Director," Yoelin added, her support of Dhu obvious in the controlled anger in her voice. As she considered Dhu's circumstances, she came to recognize what her subconscious had been telling her for the past several minutes: that she was inclined to accept Dhu's request for help. Her next question emerged in a tone just short of a growl. "Also, how the *hell* did she come to be identified as the woman you described to me?"

Exeter gave her a curious look. "As you say, your contract is fulfilled," he said, a note of suspicion in his tone. "Why the continued interest in her disposition?"

"I'm right here," Dhu said, annoyed. "Stop talking around me."

Yoelin smiled warmly at her before turning back to Exeter. "She has engaged me as her guardian angel," she said. "So I will have your responses to her questions and mine. What is her status? How is she involved in this, whatever it is? I'll add a stipulation of my own,

Director. If you cannot satisfy me with answers, I will consider her disinvolved immediately, and I will regard any subsequent attempt to interfere with her as hostile action."

Exeter's eyes widened. "You would take up arms against *me?*"

"If necessary, Director," Yoelin said evenly. "You're aware of the conditions under which I work. That's why you engaged me to begin with."

"She's a serious guardian angel," said Stefan, to Dhu.

Dhu nodded. "I get that," she whispered.

The young woman arrived with beverages, and set them on the table, withdrawing discreetly.

Yoelin eyed her until she had gone inside the bungalow and closed the door behind her. "Director?" she prodded, sampling her drink.

He licked his lips. "I don't have all the answers," he told her.

"Let's hear the ones you do have," she said.

Exeter seemed to consider his response. Finally he gave a little nod, and took a sip of gin. His glance took in Yoelin and Dhu. "I need both of you to understand that when I engaged you, Yoelin, the information I gave you was accurate to my knowledge. I have since learned, through various sources, that the 'legend' attributed to Manohra Dhu was in fact contrived. There is no such person as described. I believe the legend was set to make anyone who came for her believe that she was dangerous."

"Why?" Yoelin threw in, as Exeter paused for breath.

"Obviously, so they would shoot first and take names later," snapped Dhu.

"Crude," agreed Exeter, "but yes, essentially."

Yoelin gave him a hard look. "Then you must have suspected something amiss from the start," she said. "Because you know I don't shoot first; I'll mark my targets, yes, but I'll wait to fire until I have to. You didn't want me to bust in on Morning Dhu here and take her out unless it was absolutely necessary. That's why you didn't send an in-house operative to Havelox Rest. He might well have brought back her body, figuring that to be the simplest resolution to the tasking."

"I'll admit to a misgiving or two," Exeter conceded. "But I also knew you would be able to deal with eventualities. So many of our operatives have a tendency toward literal interpretations of their orders. I blame an education system that teaches them concretes without showing them how to gather them into abstracts." He took another, longer sip of gin. "But that's an argument for some other venue."

"We're still back to why," Yoelin pressed.

"Oh," Dhu said softly. "Oh, my."

Breath bated, Yoelin turned to her.

"It's the crippies," Dhu whispered. "They're telepathic. This rogue group you spoke of, if the crippies learned that they had had something to do with my death, they would withhold all cooperation. I had to be killed by someone they didn't want the crippies to cooperate with."

"Crippies?" asked Exeter.

Yoelin shook her head, cutting him off. "No, no, whoever shot at us at the market was part of that group."

"You don't actually know that," said Stefan.

"I think it was and it wasn't," said Exeter. "Probably he was someone associated in some way with Corporatia Security, possibly retired, and hired by the group. Again: *crippies*?"

"She just told you all you need to know about them at this point, Director," said Yoelin. She leaned forward, just a little, for emphasis. "We have a more critical problem to address first: your security."

Exeter's eyebrows lifted. "*My* security?"

Yoelin glared at him. "Don't pretend to be surprised. They already assaulted your estate. I doubt they'd have taken that measure without approaching you first to negotiate. That means you knew they'd be coming. It also means you knew about them *before* you engaged me."

Exeter raised a placating hand. "Yoelin—."

"Go to hell, Director," she fumed, and started to rise.

"Please," he said.

The magic word. Try as she might to get to her feet, she found it irresistible.

"Damn you," she whispered, reseating herself. A glance at Dhu gave her a measure of consolation—she had been about to leave as well; so, for that matter, had Stefan. She had some moral support, at least. "I'll give you one minute," she said tersely.

"No, I didn't tell you everything," Exeter admitted, measuring his words. "I did not want to prejudice what you might observe, what you might learn. I wanted to see whether your assessment dovetailed with my own, and that of several others. Thirty seconds?"

Yoelin nodded. "About that."

"Corporatia Security has been able to track several key individuals who are involved in this conspiracy," he continued, speaking faster now. "Without hard evidence, they are untouchable."

"Meaning highly-placed," said Stefan.

"Just so," said Exeter. "We learned very little from covert surveillance, but one indicator stood out: they have, or think they have, a weapon that CorpSec cannot counter. They are not yet in control of it. Once they gain control, they'll strike. Ten seconds?"

"And counting," said Yoelin.

"You're right about the attack on my estate being a punctuation on the negotiations," he said. "They want access to our personnel files, to see who can be turned and who needs to be . . . removed."

"Eliminated," Stefan amended.

The young blonde woman named Danelle returned to the table and inquired after refills and finger food. As she bent to pick up Exeter's drink, Ellie's voice suffused Yoelin's mind, piercing her thoughts like a streak of lightning. The message Ellie transmitted was so intense and urgent that Yoelin shot to her feet, hands to her head, as if in pain. The others stared at her in bewilderment.

The message ended, Yoelin took several deep breaths, and gradually took her hands away. The scene before her was bleary, as if she were observing it from under water. Like an Impressionist's painting, she thought dimly. Stefan had already started to rise, one arm extended as if to keep her from falling. Dhu simply gaped at her. Exeter's right hand had dropped to his side, and she had no doubt he was about to grasp a weapon he had cached under the chair seat. The blonde woman, Danelle, was frowning . . .

Yoelin yanked the Kreisler free and aimed it at her.

017

"Yoelin?" said Exeter, very softly. "What are you doing?"

She ignored him. What had begun as a conference to share information and make inquiries had all too abruptly metamorphosed into a life-and-death confrontation. As far as she could determine, Danelle was unarmed, although she could only examine her from the front. Stefan had a one-eighty field of view.

"Is she carrying a weapon back there, Stefan?" she asked.

Stefan's eyes went up and down. "Hmm," he mused.

"Stefan!"

"Sorry. No, nothing visible."

"You didn't have to look *that* closely," she groused. To Exeter, she added, without taking her eyes off Danelle, "How long has she been working for you, Director?"

"About a month. Yoelin—."

The woman shifted position slightly. Yoelin aimed the sidearm at her nose.

"I'd like you alive," she told Danelle. "But I wouldn't call it a necessity. Stand up, Stefan, and back well away from the chair."

He did so. Yoelin made a tiny motion with the Kreisler. "Sit down," she ordered the woman.

Danelle did not move.

With a sigh of impatience Yoelin shifted her aim lower and fired the Kreisler. The blue beam skimmed across the outside of Danelle's thigh, just above the knee. Danelle grunted in pain, but did not cry out. The wound failed to draw blood, but a red line marked the site of the beam's passing.

With a look of vile hatred for Yoelin, she sat down, legs crossed at the knees, hands folded in her lap. Her pale eyes said, "Now what?"

"En route to Havelox Rest, I got pinged," Yoelin explained. "In orbit around Rest, I learned from the douane clerk that an inquiry had been made earlier as to whether I had arrived. The query was unidentified, so I knew it couldn't be you, Director." She stared hard at Danelle. "I imagine that would have been you," she probed.

"I don't know what you're talking about," she said, through clenched teeth.

"I'm sure the director here has substances that will elicit more useful responses."

Danelle shrugged. Yoelin picked up her glass of gin and tonic and sloshed the contents onto the red line on Danelle's thigh. A scream of pain and a vicious curse followed.

"We don't want that to become infected," said Yoelin.

Exeter studied Danelle briefly, then turned to Yoelin. "I have to ask how you know all this."

Tell him.

"Hush, Ellie," whispered Yoelin. Then: "As Morning here said, Director, the crippies are telepathic. I seem to be bonded with one of them, provisionally named Ellie—."

Provisionally?

Yoelin felt a light wave of wry humor, and grinned. "And a moment ago she told me not to trust Danelle, adding, and I quote, 'she's one of *them.*'"

Exeter's eyes widened. "She, this Ellie, told you that? Just a moment ago? Telepathically?"

"Yes," Yoelin said simply.

"You're in contact with her now?" asked Dhu, her face animated. "Is she all right? Are they all right?"

Yoelin brushed her questions aside. Exeter said, "Yoelin, I find that hard to credit."

He is currently engaged in negotiations to purchase a painting called The Night Café.

Yoelin nodded. "I know the piece," she said softly. "It's one of Van Gogh's."

Exeter started. "What did you say?"

"Are they okay?" Dhu pressed.

"Have you taken possession of *The Night Café* yet, Director?" asked Yoelin.

Now his eyes rounded. "*How—?*"

"They're telepathic, Director. And telepathy is instantaneous, and as thorough as they choose to be." A flash of insight momentarily blinded her. Blinking, she sought out Exeter again. "If they can control the crippies somehow," she added, "they can use them to find out what you know. They don't need to negotiate with you."

Exeter pressed his hands to his head as if to block telepathic reading.

Yoelin laughed. "That won't help, Director," she said softly. "It doesn't work like that. In fact, I don't know how it works. That's Morning's department." She threw in a gentle nudge. "So you might want to stay on her good side, right?"

He glanced at Danelle. "And . . . her?"

Yoelin shrugged, mildly astonished that he would even ask. "That's your department, Director."

Danelle shot to her feet, dumping the table and its contents onto Exeter. He managed to spill his chair to one side to avoid a direct impact. She turned as if to flee. Stefan took a step forward just as Yoelin fired. The blue beam struck Danelle in the left side of her neck, exploding the carotid artery. A shower of blood drops followed her as she tumbled onto the patio, face down. Still alive for the moment, she groped for the wound and pressed a hand to it. Blood continued to weep through her fingers.

Yoelin dropped to a knee beside Danelle. For a moment she debated whether to roll her over, and while she hesitated, the air seemed to go out of the woman. Slack flesh fitted itself to the patio stones.

"Regrettable," said Exeter, now standing. "You could have aimed to wound."

Yoelin shook her head. "She has a weapon around here somewhere, sir. You'll recall she did not turn toward the bungalow, although I'd guess she has at least one inside. And there was no guarantee a wound would have stopped her. You saw how she took it when I fired on her the first time." She sighed, and rose to her feet. "I'll expect my payment, Director," she said, tucking the Kreisler away. "And you can use your authority to take care of this . . . mess, if you would."

"It will be done. Yoelin—."

She chopped air with her hand, cutting him off. "We're quits, Director."

"She stays here, Yoelin," said Exeter, indicating Dhu.

"Dhu leaves with me."

"Us," Stefan amended.

"Stop talking about me as if I'm not here," Dhu yelled. "I'll make *my own* decisions."

Yoelin smiled indulgently. "Once we're off this naked rock," she said, "I'll drop you off wherever you want."

"Havelox Rest."

Yoelin hesitated. "That might not be the best place for you just yet," she advised. "Not until we've resolved this."

"But—."

"Look, you engaged me to protect you," said Yoelin, with some asperity. "That means I decide how best to do that."

Exeter flipped his chair over and tore a sidearm free, tape and all. "I'm afraid I cannot allow this," he said. "And no, Yoelin, you're not quick enough, not against a weapon already drawn and aimed."

"This is a really bad idea, sir."

Exeter's brief smile said he agreed with her. "I don't see any other choice. They want Dhu . . . you, young woman. Corporatia cannot afford to let them have you."

Yoelin measured distances and angles. Exeter was standing two meters away, slightly to her left, with nothing in between them. The angle meant that she would have to aim the Kreisler across her body, a move that would cost her a precious split second, the difference between life and death. In the extreme, she might make the attempt. This was not the time.

She allowed herself to relax. "What do you want, Director?"

"The same as you. A resolution."

"You engaged to keep me safe," Dhu groused.

Yoelin turned to her, subtly changing the angle between herself and Exeter. "And you're in no danger here," she told Dhu. "Quite the opposite, I should think, now that the mole has been neutralized."

"I need to be with my crippies," Dhu said stiffly. "And I'd like to get my clothes back on."

Her combat alignment with Exeter improved, Yoelin looked at him and waited. Her taut nerves set her teeth on edge as she began the mental countdown that would end with his death or hers.

For several seconds Exeter returned her gaze. Finally, with a little shrug, he laid his weapon on the nearby chair. "What do you propose?" he asked.

She acknowledged his tacit surrender with a curt nod of her head, and allowed herself an inward sigh of relief. "I have a couple of angles I can play, sir," she told him. "Earlier you said you were keeping track of their hierarchy. I suggest you round them up, evidence or not. If nothing else, that should disorganize them sufficiently so that we can return to Havelox Rest."

"Runchal will stake us out on anthills," objected Stefan.

"That," Yoelin said grimly, "is *my* department. Well, sir?"

018

In her stateroom aboard the *Sequana*, with the spaceskiff on its way back to Havelox Rest, Yoelin sat on her bunk taking slow, deep breaths, not so much to calm herself as to allow an inner peace to develop. The confrontation with Exeter had depleted her emotional reserves. She had not been certain he would forego firing his weapon at her; in his place, she herself would not have hesitated. As the scenario had developed, she had managed to shift to a better position in which to draw and fire her Kreisler, one in which, given her superior quickness, the odds favored her. Still and all, she was glad she had not been forced to complete the maneuver.

Briefly she considered her two passengers. When she had left them for the stateroom, Stefan had been seated in the starboard captain's chair with his sketchbook and several pencils, composing her from memory in various perspectives. His expression had been focused and intense. Manohra Dhu, fully dressed now, had repaired to the galley for a cup of tea. She had nothing to say when Yoelin passed her along the gangway on the way to her stateroom.

With the *Sequana* safely ensconced in N-space, the euphoria of having survived an armed confrontation defaulted to a solemn gloom that invited a parade of memories from her dark past. The image of the hut where she had spent much of her childhood failed to disquiet her; that battle, she had already won. Other skirmishes lurked, and while she sat on the bunk, the events following her escape from the cargo ship dissolved the inner peace she sought before it had a chance to envelop her.

***

The old brick building had a window open at ground level, and she managed to pry the screen loose and squirm through the opening. Mesh tore at her bare legs as she spilled inside and fell a meter to the hard, cold floor. Had someone heard the impact? She held her breath, listening. The room was dark, lit only by filtered sunlight through the windows. But the panes themselves were clean, as if someone periodically cared for the place, whatever it was.

She peered into the shadows and saw great walls looming. Cautiously she got to her feet and approached one of them. It consisted of shelves arranged back-to-back, with a little space between them. The shelves held books; their musty odor made her nose wrinkle. She pulled one from a middle shelf and tried to puzzle out the words on the cover, but *Fauna of Skadany* meant nothing to her. She had no need of books at the moment. She needed something to eat, and a safe place to stay.

Gradually it occurred to her that if she crawled onto the bottom shelves of the back-to-backs, and nudged some of the books out of the way, she might insert herself there and at least get some sleep. A stack of three books made a makeshift pillow. She closed her eyes.

When she opened them again, a man older than her father was staring down at her.

***

Yoelin shivered, though Abnoba maintained the stateroom at a pleasant 295K. The man's name rumbled across her memories like a thunder cloud: Marton Gotsch. He had been kind enough at first, even generous, sharing his meals and offering her a bunk of her own while he tended the library, as it was called. Over the next few years he encouraged her to read, and tutored her in the sciences and in history, and taught her to assist him in his caretaking of the library.

Her countenance darkened, remembering.

When she turned thirteen, he began to tutor her in what he told her was the profession of courtesan. If she were skillful enough, she might in time become wealthy, with access to power beyond her reckoning. His words. At first she tolerated the lessons, uncomfortable though they were and even frightening, because she feared even more being abandoned if she did not learn them. She did not care for any of it, but over time she came to understand what she was to do, and how to do it, and how to pretend she took pleasure in what she was doing.

When she turned sixteen, Gotsch assigned her temporarily to a corporate hierarch, introduced to her as Carpy Diam, which she immediately recognized as fictitious. Freed for the moment from

Gotsch's direct control, she wondered whether she might find a way to get away completely. That possibility was scotched when she realized that the hierarch was keeping ultra-close tabs on her, as if he had been warned in advance that she might try to escape.

She bided her time, and continued her general education. She logged other assignments, none of long duration, and lost herself in learning whenever possible, to take her mind off what she was being forced to do.

When she was eighteen, she found herself in the company of a young man named Paul Wroclawski, a hierarch's son. Wroclawski took one look at her, and sat her down beside him on his bed, and apologized to her. She was so astounded that she broke down into tears, and spent the next hour or so wailing into his shoulder and chest. Dimly she recalled that he had spoken to her in the softest of voices during that time, but even now she had no idea what he had actually said.

In the stateroom she said, "Paul," keeping her voice low, though Abnoba could detect even the faintest breath of a whisper.

Paul Wroclawski had entered into a marriage of convenience with the daughter of another hierarch. She soon found more suitable companionship, and he, after considerable anguish, had asked his father for advice.

Until that time, Yoelin had not been introduced by name, and none of her clients had thought to ask, being content with endearments that ranged from benign to downright malignant. After her tears had diminished to a trickle, and with Paul's arms still protectively around her, he inquired after her name.

In the stateroom, Yoelin sighed. *The moment of my birth*, she thought.

Paul's question had given her a glimpse of light, a glimmer of hope. Just as her escape from the shipping crate had done. Yoelin, she told him. Yoelin Thibbony.

Later she came to grasp that he assumed she was a bastard child, discarded by the well-to-do family. But that was later.

He had apologized once again, and she shook her head, telling him it was all right. He spoke to her of his marital circumstances, and asked about her own status. Uncertain, she simply said that she would have to go back when he was done with her.

"However long that might be," he told her, smiling.

She did not know what he meant.

"Your tears tell me the true story," he explained. "I don't know how long I can protect you. I'll tell my father that you are just what I needed, and I'll keep you on as long as I can. For the sake of appearances, you'd better room with me. I'll get you a bed—I'll say that I snore loudly afterwards, and that you needed a place to retreat to. It's almost true, by the way; I've heard my father sound like a ruptured ship's motor."

She laughed, despite herself.

"Yoelin . . . I think I can arrange to free you, even from under my father's watchful eyes. It may take a spot of time. He'll be angry. He paid quite a sum to, er, rent you, and he'll lose his deposit. But I think I can . . . *no*, I *will* do this."

She squeezed her eyes shut, and opened them again. "I'm scared."

"I can teach you ways to protect yourself," he promised. "You won't like them; they'll involve bruises and scrapes, and maybe even a fracture or two. They won't prevent you from being afraid, but they will give you confidence that you can deal with whatever—or *who*ever—is frightening you."

In the stateroom, she smiled as she heard her simple, plaintive question. *How?*

"I hold black belts in aikido and jiu-jitsu," he had told her. "And I'm rather good at *savate*."

In the stateroom, Yoelin glanced at the wardrobe, set into the bulkhead. The door was closed, but she knew the exact location of her *gi*, the white cotton outfit now pale gray with years of lessons and practice at various dojos, and of her two black belts. She rubbed her left forearm, and the round, slightly puckered scar where the bone had punched through.

Some hundred days later, she had accompanied him to Verveine, to the lavish hotel overlooking the lake in the mountains, and there he gave her the news that frightened her the most.

"This will be the last day we are together, Yoelin," he told her, as they stood on the fifth-level balcony and smelled the fresh, cool air wafting over the water.

"But what of you?" she worried.

"My father told me before we left that I had to keep up appearances." He smiled grimly. "Apparently he feels that I have dallied or tarried with you for too long. He has advised me that he intends to terminate your lease upon our return."

"You deserve better, Paul."

He gave her an arch look. "You, perhaps?"

She shrugged away and turned around, her rigid spine to him. "Ye gods, no. Don't even think that."

"Yoelin."

"What?" she snapped. Turning back around, she put an apology into her tone. "What?" she asked gently.

"You can be whatever you choose."

She chuckled. "*Such* a cliché."

"Life *is* a cliché, Yoelin. Evil has been done; now it's time for you to do some good."

In the stateroom, she recalled the touch of his fingers upon her cheek.

"Goodbye, Yoelin," he said.

"You mean . . . you mean *now*?"

In the stateroom, she recalled her dry mouth, her tongue moistening her lips.

"But I thought . . . ," she stammered. "I thought we . . ."

"Now that *would* be a cliché," he said.

"Oh, I don't care, Paul, I don't care." She paused for a moment, thinking. "You said goodbye. Does that mean I am free now?"

"It does."

"You said it's our last day together. And our last night?"

He took a step away from her. "Yoelin, no."

"If I am free, then I am free to *offer*, and to *give*."

In the stateroom, she recalled the tender, stricken look in his eyes. It told her everything she needed to know.

"Oh, no," she had whispered. "I did *not* see that coming. Oh,

Paul. Poor Paul."

"So you see, I can't. The memory would be too . . ."

"Good?" she supplied. "Intense?"

His eyes laughed at her, but his face was sober. "I was thinking painful."

"The point is, Paul, you would have the memory. We both would. Something for you and me to fall back on, whenever darkness comes."

"*Such* a—."

In the stateroom, she could still feel his lips moving under the cover of her hand.

His surrender came as a sigh. "Last night, then."

In the stateroom, she allowed herself a glimpse or two of the night they had passed. She was unable to find words that adequately described what she now felt, looking back. Regret, of course, always that, though its direction was nameless. What, exactly, was there to regret? She had made the offer freely, and freely he had accepted, and she was glad of that fact. Longing? But even in the throes—and there definitely had been a throe or two—she had known and accepted that this was a man she could not have. In any event, she did not envision a sessile life for herself. No, the feeling was something akin to contentment. She was glad to have passed that night, and she was glad to have passed it with him.

In the subsequent years, she did not look him up or try to see him, and she ignored the urges—less frequent as the years went by— to find out what had become of him. It was not quite enough that they had passed that night together; not quite, but it was all they were to have.

She folded her hands in her lap and leaned back against the bulkhead. She had resolved her fear of the hut by being the agent of its destruction. Paul Wroclawski had had a hand in resolving the abuse of her years of confinement, and in any event there was not much she could do about those years except move on . . .

Well, there was one thing . . .

It involved Paul. In the morning, he had given her a name and a location, the title and operational codes to a spacecraft, and a fundscard to an account bearing more money than she had ever heard of. The name was Dannik Exeter, the location Providence. And there was Paul's accompanying recommendation . . .

Five years later, she returned to the library, intent on mayhem. She found Marton Golsch in his cubbyhole, busily dusting old tomes, coughing and hacking in the resultant cloud. Shrunken, smaller than she remembered, he reeked of tobacco and cheap rye. She stood gazing at him dispassionately. It took him almost half a minute to recognize her. When he did, he backed up against a wall, his hands protectively in front of him. Words failed him; he began to blubber, choking on his pleas. She laughed at him, and told him he was not worth the little effort it would take to kill him. She had walked away then, and not looked back.

In the stateroom, she let her mind go blank. The memories of Paul slowly faded away, and with them the sense of loss she still felt, now and then. Now Stefan Coppenrath had tumbled inadvertently from out of her past back into her life. She had agreed to pose for him at the end of her present Rescue, but what of beyond that? Of a certainty he was the first man since Paul for whom she felt an attraction. But for that attraction to mean anything, her living arrangements had to stabilize. She might have to remain in one place for far longer than she ever had since gaining her freedom. Her fear of that was tantamount to a phobia.

"I wonder what it would be called," she muttered, gazing absently at her boots. "Domophobia? Fear of having a home?"

And what do I tell Stefan of Deirdre Hanratty? she wondered. *I'm not that little girl anymore; I can't be. Losing her was part of my own Rescue. My life, Yoelin's life, began the night Paul rescued me. How can I go back to be Deirdre,* how?

"No," she whispered, shaking her head. "I can't go back, not even for Stefan."

Yes you can.

Yoelin started, and sat up straight, eyes wide. Where had that come from? What within her had contradicted her claim? Most of all . . . most of all, what did it mean?

"How?" she asked.

She heard no response.

"How?" she cried.

"You are distraught," said Abby. *"You should get some rest."*

"I will, I will," mumbled Yoelin. *Ellie,* she thought, *are you there?*

Always. We are bonded, you and I.

Yoelin felt as if a weight had been lifted from her shoulders. "Was that you?" she asked, aloud.

No, that came from within you. But I think I understand it.

"Tell me!"

It is better that you find your own way to who you are.

"How can I tell him, Ellie?"

No answer came.

"Ellie, please," she moaned.

Ponder the butterfly, Yoelin.

She gasped, puzzled and uncertain. "I don't understand, Ellie."

It will come to you. I agree with your computer: you should rest.

"Ellie . . ."

For several minutes Yoelin waited for more from Ellie. At last she concluded that nothing more would be forthcoming for now. After removing her boots, she stretched out on her bunk, and fell asleep wondering whether she would be able to fall asleep.

019

Yoelin jerked awake to noise that soon resolved itself into a signal of incoming communication. She sat up, rubbing her eyes. "Off," she muttered, and took a few breaths, steadying herself.

"Who is it, Abby?" she finally asked, alert now.

"Dannik Exeter."

Yoelin's brow knit. "Well, put him on."

A door in the opposite bulkhead slid open to reveal a monitor in which Exeter's face and shoulders appeared. He was wearing a dark blue shirt, and Yoelin concluded he was no longer on Ouvert.

"Many of the ringleaders have been rounded up," he announced without preamble. "We're still trying to locate the others. Corporatia wants heads to roll, but we used that very fact as leverage in our interrogations. You'd be surprised to learn how talkative they were." He hesitated briefly, and added, "Yoelin, I think you had better cancel whatever you were planning to do on Havelox Rest."

"Why?"

Exeter's lips puffed out with his sigh. "Corporatia is going to annex the planet. They will not allow those crippies to be used against them under any circumstances."

"I think that would be a very bad idea, Director," she replied. "In your position, I would discourage the hierarchs from taking any such action. I'd leave Rest strictly alone."

He stared hard at her. "You aren't seriously considering a Rescue of the crippies."

That won't be necessary.

"That won't be necessary, Director. I'd advise Corporatia not to try to find out *why* it won't be necessary."

"I'll pass on your, ah, thoughts," said Exeter, scowling. He looked at her sharply for a moment, and went on, "One other matter of interest, regarding the woman Danelle. After you departed from Ouvert, I had the grounds and bungalow searched thoroughly. No weapons were found anywhere except those that I had emplaced.

During interrogation, the ringleaders were asked about her, and none of them had any idea who she was. I believe them; they would have given her up in a finger-snap if it would help them."

"I . . . don't understand."

"It's nice to see you nonplussed for a change, Yoelin."

She dismissed this with a quick shake of her head. "Forget that. Who the hell was she, then?"

"We are still not certain," Exeter answered. "We're searching her listed residence on Scarletta, which she owned under the name Danelle Moths." He glanced at her as if to ask whether the name rang any bells. When she did not respond, he continued, "Many of her records and communications are encrypted with a very good security device. It's going to take some time to break them down. It appears that she was a freelance locator; she found people, for a fee. Something like your line of work, I believe."

"I have heard that name," she acknowledged, after a moment. "But our paths never crossed, professionally or personally. I couldn't tell you anything about her. Why was she looking for you?"

"That's just it. She was not looking for me. A preliminary check of her recent activities indicates that she was looking for *you*."

Aghast, Yoelin slowly got to her feet. "She *what*?"

"We're going over her records and movements, to see if we can find out who hired her to find you. For the moment, I don't have any more information to pass on. But I think you should keep in mind that someone is looking for you."

She nodded absently, still shocked. "Yes. Yes, of course."

"Danelle had a sister, Velanne Moths, in the same line of work," added Exeter. "You might keep an eye out for her as well." His expression grew somber and apologetic. "Unfortunately, the information regarding Danelle's demise became a matter of public record before we learned of the relationship. We've closed it off and classified it, but it might already be too late."

Yoelin shrugged helplessly. Rescues were rarely simple projects, even if the wording was as clear as crystal. After a moment, she returned her gaze to the monitor again. "Hang about. Why would Danelle come to you, then? And if she's been with you for a month, that means—."

"I'll be in touch," said Exeter, and vanished.

After the monitor closed, Yoelin sat back down, mouth agape, scarcely able to credit what she had just heard. If what he had told her was accurate, she had shot and killed someone who was merely trying to find her. But Ellie had said . . .

She reached out to Ellie, and tried not to put too much accusation into her tone. "Ellie, you told me she was one of them."

She was hired by a hierarch.

And Ellie did not yet distinguish between corporate hierarchs, she thought. "I think I see," she said slowly, a bit of light shining through. "All right, who? Which one?"

The identity was hidden from me. It is possible she did not know. She may have been hired by proxy.

Yoelin nodded, though Ellie could not see it. "Sometimes that is the procedure. Danelle Moths . . . I wonder. Abby . . ." She fell silent for a moment, uncertain.

". . . Taps foot impatiently, waiting."

"What? Um . . . no, belay that."

"As you wish."

Yoelin drummed her fingers on the sleeping pad, and stopped when she realized that she was in effect tapping her foot impatiently. Finally she asked, "Abby, how much longer to Havelox Rest?"

"Twenty nine point seven . . . thirty minutes."

Time enough, thought Yoelin, for a shower.

***

Lathered up, Yoelin stood away from the shower spray and ordered it off, deep in thought and memory. Moments earlier, she had been about to ask Abnoba to turn up a point of contact for Paul Wroclawski, only to reject the notion that had occurred to her. In the shower, however, thoughts of him had recurred, and with it the possibility that he had hired Danelle Moths. As unlikely as it sounded to her, it was nevertheless worth investigating, even if only to eliminate that possibility.

"Abby, raise Paul Wroclawski," she said, as she began to apply the scrubbie to the lather.

"You told me never to contact him."

Yoelin sighed. "Just do it, Abby."

"You were very specific and adamantine—."

"Abnoba! Now!"

"Arightaright. Untwist your knickers."

Scant seconds later, Yoelin heard a voice as familiar to her as if she had just spoken with him yesterday.

"Yoel—. Ye gods, you look—."

"Abnoba," yelled Yoelin. "I said nothing about visual. Belay visual!"

Paul's laughter reminded her of happier moments. "I turned my back," he told her.

"Of course you did."

"Truly. Truly, Yoelin." A second later, he added, "It looks shut off. I must say, this is a pleasant surprise in some ways."

Yoelin stopped scrubbing for a moment. "Some?"

"It's been . . . a long time, Yoelin," said Paul, his tone quiet and pensive. "Under the circumstances—our circumstances—I can only surmise that there is trouble in the wind. You've broken a well-constructed silence to approach me."

"You answered commo right away," Yoelin pointed out.

"I will always answer your commos right away."

"Oh, Paul . . ."

Briefly he seemed lost for words, too. Finally he said, "Unfortunately, my personal situation has not altered in the interim. Nor do I expect it to anytime soon."

"I suppose not."

Another silence followed, this one longer. Yoelin stopped bathing, and stood very still in the stall. Head down and eyes closed, she remembered . . .

"Yoelin," said Paul, gently altering the moment. "You did commo me."

She blinked herself back to the present. "I just had a question, Paul, but it's important. As you don't have my contact data, you have no way of getting to me. So: did you hire anyone to find me? A locater named Danelle Moths, specifically?"

143

His response came readily enough. "No, not at all. But I've heard the name."

"Well, scratch her off your ready list," said Yoelin.

"I . . . see. May I ask what happened?"

She lowered her eyes. "It's . . . complicated. At the time, given what I knew, killing her was in order. Given what I now know, not so much. I'm trying to find out who hired her, and for what purpose. Exeter's working on it, but her records are very encrypted."

"I can ask around," Paul offered. "See what turns up."

"No, Paul," said Yoelin. "This is my kind of business."

"I'll keep that in mind when I ask around."

"If you learn something . . ."

"I will," he said. He hesitated. Then: "Yoelin? How's that shower?"

She barked a laugh. "What? Why?"

"I . . . have thought of you . . ."

"I know what you mean," she admitted. "What's that to do with my bathing? Okay, perhaps that's not the best question to ask."

"Well . . ."

Ask me, she thought, and cast that thought at him. *Just ask me.*

She prodded him. "Shyness does not become you, Paul."

"I have no right . . . Yoelin, I'm glad you got in touch. If I find out anything—."

"Abnoba," said Yoelin, cutting him off. "Enable visual."

***

"Abby," said Yoelin, dressed once more and seated on the berth, "where are Stefan and Morning?"

"Stefan continues to sketch on the bridge, and Morning Dhu is asleep in the other stateroom."

She breathed a little sigh of relief at the direct response; she had no desire to engage in banter with a computer trying to distill its own personality. At the same time, she suspected Abby was toying with her, like a cat in a yarn kiosk.

"How much longer to Havelox Rest?"

"We are already in orbit around Havelox Rest, out of range of their sensors, as you instructed."

"You might have announced our arrival," Yoelin said peevishly.

"Should I have interrupted your . . . bathing?"

Yoelin rolled her eyes. "Ye gods. Very well, maintain orbit."

"Maintaining."

Yoelin got up and went to the bridge, where Stefan was bent over a sketch, unaware of her arrival. On the deck around him lay several wadded pieces of sketch paper. He looked up when she cleared her throat for attention.

"Not going well?" she asked him, peering over his shoulder.

Stefan shrugged, and flipped a few sheets back over. "One or two useful pieces," he replied. "I'm just putting together some pose concepts."

"One of which, it seems, is based on an inspiration from Ouvert."

She noted he had the grace to look sheepish.

"Occasionally I paint or draw for my own enjoyment," he said.

Yoelin sat down. "Abby, wake Morning Dhu and have her come up to the bridge, please."

"Waking. She's . . . she threw a boot at me!"

Yoelin grimaced. "Abby, just . . . just pass on the message."

"Council of war?" inquired Stefan.

She nodded.

"I take it you have a plan in mind," he said.

"Plan enough." She looked up as Dhu arrived on the bridge and took a seat on a pull-down bench, sullen and still sleepy. "We can't be certain of the situation on the ground," Yoelin went on. "Perhaps Stefan is right, and Runchal is on the lookout for all of us. But I got us into this mess. Runchal might be satisfied with just me, leaving you two . . ." She paused to regard Dhu. "With any luck," she told her, "you'll be able to care for your crippies again."

The news did not brighten Dhu. "Finally," she said, glum.

"I don't think I'm going to like this next bit," said Stefan.

"You're not," agreed Yoelin. "I'm going down there and disembark. Abby will whisk you back into orbit. You'll await developments. If you haven't heard from me in two days, the *Sequana* is yours. I'll instruct Abby to make the transfer." She turned to Dhu before he could respond. "You'll have to decide, under that circumstance, whether you want to return to Rest. If you do, Stefan will drop you off; otherwise, he will take you to wherever you want to go. You may, of course, elect to remain on board with him."

Dhu cast a morose glance at him. "Hardly," she said.

"You have every right to be upset," said Yoelin. "At least you're alive so you can be upset."

"Don't be so smug," Dhu shot back. "You didn't have to do this to me."

"You're right, I didn't have to," Yoelin conceded. "I could have left you at the market and fled on my own. Perhaps you'd still be alive; perhaps you wouldn't." She got to her feet and started walking around the bridge. "But you *are* alive. And aside from some embarrassment on Ouvert, you are unharmed."

"What *are* you going to do?" Stefan asked her.

"I'm going to walk right into *The Rutting Skull* and give myself up."

Stefan was aghast. "You can't do that."

"He'll feed you to the catfish in Squabble Lake," added Dhu.

Yoelin paused to grin at her. "I didn't think you'd care," she said.

"I don't. I mean, I do. I mean—."

Yoelin held a hand up. "He won't expect me to surrender," she said.

"You hope," Stefan put in.

"I hope, yes. I hope I have time to get a few words off. Perhaps even a phrase. If I am allowed to say that much, I might get him to hear me out before he makes a precipitate decision."

"You hope," Stefan said again.

"The only other option," said Yoelin, seating herself back in the captain's chair, "is to leave here and never come back. Any of us."

"But your assignment is over," Dhu pointed out. "You're risking your life for nothing."

Yoelin smiled easily. "You hired me for a Rescue," she reminded Dhu. "The Rescue is still on."

"But—."

"Besides," Yoelin went on, "I have an ally."

"You hope," said Dhu.

020

Once on the ground, Yoelin felt less confident about her chances. The scant relief of knowing that Stefan and Dhu were safely back in orbit failed to balance the uncertainty of persuading Runchal to hear her out. Ellie might or might not intercede for her; as yet Yoelin had received no telepathic communication from her. Tension knotted her shoulders as she made her way past the jetties for *The Rutting Skull*, no longer inviting her inside for a drink, but looming now—a brooding, shadowy structure even in broad daylight. It looked now as if it might hold a dungeon and a medieval torture chamber. She shivered, eyeing it as she approached.

Around her, a few people tied up boats or pulled various types of maintenance, and paid her little attention. She had no fear of being recognized by them. As a precautionary measure Runchal would have advised only his sons and his security personnel to be on the lookout for her, and would have given them her description. Yoelin doubted he actually expected her to return.

She drew up to the oaken door of the tavern. The pounding of her heart throbbed inside her head, and for just a moment a waft of dizziness staggered her. Uncertain of her reception, she hoped to find Runchal within, supervising the operation of the tavern. If she could just get in a few words before he ordered her silenced and fed to the catfish, she might yet rescue the day. Summoning courage, she recovered her balance, and tugged the door open.

The interior was the same as she remembered it from her previous visit. She looked about for Runchal, but he evidently had duties elsewhere. A wry smile creased her face as she wondered whether he was even now seeing to the catfish in Squabble Lake, in anticipation of her return. The smile faded as she realized that Runchal's oldest son, Boltory, now stood behind the counter and looked as if he had been waiting for her to arrive.

Dismay smothered her heart as she realized the *Sequana* had been detected, after all. She had supposed a distance of a million kilometers to be safe. With the *Sequana*'s transponder identified, other events had been set into motion. Boltory stood now in Runchal's stead, his treachery manifest. Off to the right, near where Stefan had been sitting the first night she had come to the tavern, she spotted an armed man who almost certainly belonged to Runchal's security staff. He had yet to draw his sidearm, but his hand poised just above it. She could kill him readily enough—but she had not come to defend herself. If only Runchal were here in lieu of Boltory.

In many respects Boltory looked almost like his father, from his vast, yellow-brown mustache to his great bulk. At the present moment, he was attired in bib overalls and a blue-checked flannel shirt, partially covered by a white apron that had seen several spills. He did not smile as he regarded her.

Movement behind her added tension to her shoulders. Another security guard—she sensed his approach, and knew when he had stopped, perhaps three paces behind her. At the other end of the counter, a third guard made an appearance, coming into view from behind a post that supported the staircase.

Yoelin glanced over her shoulder and smiled at the security guard. Thin and angular, he was clearly no relative of Runchal; she was forced to assume that his loyalty—and the loyalty of the other two—went to Boltory. Not the best news, she thought, but at least no weapons had been drawn, yet. The guard moved to within reach of her, and shoved her hard enough to promise worse if she did not move in the direction he wanted.

Under other circumstances Yoelin might have responded in any one of several neutralizing maneuvers. Instead, she walked up to the counter a couple meters down from Boltory, and placed her hands on top of it, both to demonstrate that they were empty and to give them something to do. A finger went to a smear on the counter top, and she picked at it with her nail. She did not so much as glance in Boltory's direction.

"You know," he said, his tone more a statement of fact than an accusation.

The pitch of his voice was higher than Yoelin expected from so large a man. Not like his father's boomer. She wondered whether that had been a factor in his behavior.

Slowly she turned her head to look at him. He had not moved from the end of the counter, nor had the security men begun to close in on her. The threat on all sides was implicit, but that could change at any moment. She hoped it would not come to killing them, for it would not help her cause at all. Quite the contrary.

"Money?" she asked quietly.

Boltory shrugged his massive shoulders. "They offered me a position," he told her. "Better than Father offered me. He said I was not suitable to . . . to . . ." His countenance reddened as he stared at her. "How did you know?" he asked.

"May I have an ale?" she asked.

The request made Boltory laugh. It also established his control, as she intended; he could afford to be magnanimous. He moved to a spigot, set a mug under it, and filled it for her. The maneuver brought him within reach of her, and she noted that for possible use later. But with his task completed, he resumed his position at the end of the counter.

Yoelin gave him a mock toast, and took a sip. Her free hand went to a pocket of her black jeans. With the movement, the security man on her right took a step forward. She withdrew a tin and opened it, taking out a cheroot, and lighting it with the lighter from the tin.

Careful not to blow smoke in Boltory's direction, she said, "It wasn't difficult to figure. Someone here had to have passed on the data regarding the crippies. Most folks on Rest are here because they *want* to be here; they aren't going to jeopardize their freedoms or ruin the lives they've worked so hard to establish, no matter what rewards or incentives they're offered." She took a gulp and another sip from her mug, and went on, "No, the traitor had to be someone who was dissatisfied with his lot here, which meant someone who was born and raised here, and wanted something more in his life. This indeed appears to be the case." Now she looked directly at Boltory, and took another drag on her cheroot, exhaling through her nose. "Incidentally, where is Runchal?"

"Traitor," repeated Boltory. The red of his face darkened as he slammed his fist into his own chest. "*I* was the one who was betrayed!" he snarled, the pitch of his voice rising even higher with each word. "Me, the firstborn! Always the firstborn has inherited the tavern, always. He called me a disappointment. He said I was not man enough for the position." Again Boltory struck himself. "He betrayed *me*. His firstborn son."

"So you decided to enslave an entire species," Yoelin said calmly, "to a group of people who would militarize their abilities to further their own aims of power and corruption."

"I'll have a position of authority with them," Boltory declared. "They respect me. They want me with them." He picked up a sidearm from the counter and aimed it at her. "And you will not stop me. They'll be here any time now, to take over."

That's why Exeter couldn't locate the other conspirators, she thought. *They're out here in The Dragons.*

"Dragons," she murmured. "They're sea dragons."

Boltory frowned at her. "What's that?"

Yoelin waved him off. "It's not important. Boltory, I don't think you fully grasp what you're facing here. They aren't—."

"I don't want to hear it," yelled Boltory. "You're wrong!"

"And you're afraid I'm right."

Her Palmetto began to buzz. She gazed placidly at Boltory, waiting for him to decide what he wanted her to do about it. Finally she crossed her arms over her chest, and leaned aside against the counter. "Well?" she said.

Boltory hesitated, and glanced at the security men. "Answer it," he said finally. "Watch what you say. And put it on speaker, so I can hear as well."

Yoelin complied. "Go ahead, Abby."

She heard Stefan's voice immediately. "Are you all right?" he asked.

"I'm fine. What's going on?"

"It's getting crowded out here," he told her. "Four ships arrived a few moments ago. Cruiser class, I'd say. But there's something funny . . ."

"Funny guffaw, or funny odd?"

Boltory took a step closer, and keened an ear.

"Two of the ships just started operating on maneuvering thrusters," said Stefan. An edge of concern crept into his tone. "Shouldn't they be prepping for the last Track down to the surface?"

Yoelin glanced at Boltory, and tilted her head in a question. Consternation wrinkled his pale brow.

"That's the standard procedure," said Yoelin.

"Now they're . . . oh, *no*!"

"*Stefan*," she yelled. "What?"

"They just . . . they just . . . collided with a third ship," said Stefan. His voice shook. "I can't tell . . . there's not much damage, maybe they . . . there's some debris, but maybe it's not serious. I think the hulls are intact."

Boltory stepped forward and grabbed the Palmetto from her. His face looked as if he had been holding his breath for too long. "What's happening out there?" he shouted.

"Abby doesn't recognize your voice," Yoelin said. "She won't transmit."

Frustrated, Boltory made as if to cast the Palmetto to the floor.

"Uh-uh," said Yoelin. "You'll just cut off all communication." She held out her hand, palm up. "Let me have it back. I'll find out for you."

He laid the device on the counter and moved away from it. "You'd better," he warned.

Yoelin left the device where it was and simply spoke. "Can you hear me, Stefan?"

"Clear as silver bells. The fourth ship just enTracked; it's gone. I've no idea where it went, but the bow was aimed away from the planet. The other three ships are . . . I'd say they're limping away on thrusters, licking their wounds and trying to make them Track-worthy again."

Boltory's voice was pitched to a squeak. "They're leaving me?"

"It looks that way," said Yoelin.

"No!" Boltory shook his head violently. "No, this is wrong. You're lying! Kventher, kill her!"

The tavern door burst from its hinges and skidded across the floor. A great eel-like creature, gray brown and still damp, thrust

151

itself through the opening, splintering the jambs. As it slithered into the tavern, steering itself on feeble limbs, its hindquarters lashed out and cast one of the security guards into a wall. A second guard started to fire his weapon, only to have it knocked from his hand by Yoelin. The third guard turned and fled.

"Ellie," said Yoelin, smiling.

The crippy slung a pair of loops around Yoelin, and lifted its head so that it could nuzzle her face.

"I missed you, too," said Yoelin.

Sea dragon. I like that.

"What happened out there, Ellie?"

The others have seen how we can control them. They will not come back.

"I thought something like that might happen."

This one meant to kill you.

Yoelin regarded Boltory for a moment. He seemed frozen in place, unable even to breathe. His pale eyes glistened with wonder and terror.

"Ellie, where is Runchal?" she asked.

He is locked in the storage room.

Yoelin stepped out of Ellie's coils and went around the counter to the door of the storage room. An old-fashioned Yoelin Lock Company padlock secured it, and for a few seconds Yoelin squeezed her eyes shut against the return of memories. When she opened them again, her fingers sought the brass key on a nearby shelf. A moment later, she pushed the door open.

Runchal was seated on the dusty floor, bound hand and foot. His eyes rounded when Yoelin slipped the Kolal knife from her boot, and he tried to roll away from her. "Let me cut your bonds," she told him, and he relaxed, turning his body so that she might free him.

Liberated, Runchal got to his feet, rubbing his wrists and straightening his tusk pendant. He gave Yoelin a brief look of gratitude. Then, staggering at first, he made his way out to the counter, where Boltory remained immobilized. Runchal's attention, however, focused on Ellie.

"How?" he boomed.

"It's a long story," Yoelin replied

"They shouldn't stay out of the water for very long," Runchal told her. "Ten or fifteen minutes at most. They need the water to support some of their weight."

"You know about the sea dragons?" asked Yoelin.

"Most folks here do," answered Runchal. "But we don't discuss them." For several seconds he studied Boltory. At last he went on, still addressing Yoelin. "Sea dragons; as good a term as any. I suppose this one is bonded to you. They're known to do that, with those who are nice to them. Would you please ask it to release my son?"

"Ellie is a she."

Runchal nodded. "Of course."

"Ellie?" prodded Yoelin.

Boltory slumped against the counter, gasping for breath, eyes huge as he stared at Ellie.

Your friends have just arrived. In fact, here they are now.

Yoelin turned toward the doorway just as Stefan stepped through, gawking at the damage. Manohra Dhu followed, equally cautious. Her eyes lit up when she spotted Ellie. She walked over to her, and rubbed the scales on top of her head.

"Why?" Runchal asked Boltory.

Boltory glowered at him. "You said I couldn't manage the tavern after you."

"And you think your actions today will convince me otherwise?" rumbled Runchal. "You won't be the first Havelock relative who's been fed to the catfish."

Ellie began to slither toward the door. Yoelin felt affection and strength emanate from her. As the sea dragon's tail passed out of sight, Yoelin took a moment to greet Stefan with a smile—a gesture he did not return. The corners of her mouth drooped to a frown of puzzled worry. His expression suggested that something heavy weighed on his mind, and she had no idea what it might be. But she returned her attention to the two men, father and son, estranged now, and jabbing their words back and forth.

"If I may," she interrupted.

Runchal did not look around. "This is not your business,

woman," he growled.

"I beg to differ," said Yoelin. "I perform Rescues; I rescue people."

"You can't salvage him. He's beyond salvage."

"What would you know about it?" cried Boltory.

Yoelin took a step closer, addressing Runchal's broad back. "I daresay you're right. His bitter arrogance is difficult to wipe away. He'll always blame someone else for his shortcomings. Until, unless, he should learn that he can choose to do some good with his life."

"So why—?"

"Because he still has a chance," said Yoelin, and waited.

Seconds passed. Slowly, Runchal's massive shoulders relaxed. He glanced at her over his shoulder.

"Go on," he said.

"He can't work here," said Yoelin. "I understand that. But I can take him to a place where he will have a choice of difficult but rewarding labor, or."

"Or?"

Yoelin grinned without mirth. "There really isn't an 'or,'" she said.

"I see." Runchal scratched the side of his neck with the tusk while he reflected on her offer. Finally he said, "You have a ship. You'll take him with you?"

"I'm not going!" yelled Boltory.

"I don't trust him loose on my ship," Yoelin replied evenly. "Can you have him bound securely and placed in the cargo hold. He'll only be there for about ten hours. Make sure he goes before we leave."

"You *can't*," blurted Boltory.

"*Silence*," roared Runchal. "You have a choice of two careers: fish food, or with her. Start it off right, and make the best choice."

Boltory's eyes cast hatred at Runchal and Yoelin, and she was glad she had asked that the young man be bound. She didn't pity Exeter; he could deal with Boltory.

Runchal seized a sidearm and used it to motion Boltory to a bench. With the young man subdued, he summoned several security personnel, and quietly issued instructions. Yoelin paid little attention to this; her part was over.

Nearby, Dhu cleared her throat for attention. When Yoelin looked her way, Dhu said, "I think I owe you an apology."

"None necessary."

"I probably didn't make things easy for you."

Yoelin shrugged. "In your place, I would have made them difficult. Just take care of the crip . . . sea dragons. And would you please see that Ellie gets some dried fruit now and then?"

Dhu nodded. "I will. Of course I will," she said. "And . . . thank you."

Yoelin waited until Dhu had passed outside, before moving herself into the moment she was now beginning to dread. The plaintive quality of her voice pained her as she said, "Stefan?"

"I'll . . . be at my hut—well, the hut you rented—for another month or so," he said woodenly, averting his eyes from her. "I'm better there. I don't do well on board spacecraft. You saw that on the bridge. I don't even do well in here. I need scenic surroundings like this island to work well. I need . . . I need peace. That's why I got out of the business, your business. I needed peace."

She realized he was on a talking jag. But what was he trying to tell her? She kept the tears from her eyes, but not from her voice. "Stefan?"

He would not look at her. Yoelin wanted to reach out to him, to touch him, but held back. He had to find his own way; that, she could not do for him.

"It's a sedentary sort of occupation, being an artist," he said. "I can't . . . I can't move around like you do."

"I don't have to move around," she blurted. "I don't."

"I would never ask you to change your nature."

"But I'll come back," she promised. "I will pose for you."

Now he looked at her. "I would like that," he admitted, his tone neutral. "I hope it comes to pass." Abruptly he brightened. "Well, you have a trip to take, and a report to make. Go to it."

"Stefan," she said, and was unable to say more, her voice stuck in her throat. His unexpected announcement of what amounted to separation shook her. She did not know how to react, how to respond. In the end, she decided against both, and strode from the tavern, well aware that her spine was straight and erect.

Only after Boltory had been loaded onto the *Sequana* and the spaceskiff inserted into N-space did she begin to weep.

021

Yoelin's tears had dried by the time she came to stand in the atrium, still intact in the remains of Exeter's mansion on Providence. The fires were extinguished, the smoke blown away, and yet enough of the pungent smell remained that she decided to forego lighting a cheroot. Exeter had expressed an initial surprise at her announcement that the *Sequana* was parked in synchronous orbit, but invited her down nevertheless, and now he offered her a drink and a chair, both of which she accepted. For the occasion she had chosen a loose turquoise outsuit, a compromise between official and casual, and had bound back her hair in a chignon. Exeter wore slacks and a pullover of a design and quality only upper management could properly afford. She took a long sip of the single-malt whiskey—something with Glen in the name, she supposed—and set the tumbler carefully on the end table beside her.

"A present, you said," Exeter prodded, his chair facing hers three paces away.

"You're rather direct and to the point," she said.

"I thought you would appreciate that."

She ran a fingertip around the rim of the tumbler. "How is the situation on Havelox Rest shaking out?" she asked him.

He leaned back, hands curled over the chair arms, gazing at her placidly while he gathered himself. Finally he said, "There's no way to suppress the secret of Havelox Rest now, Yoelin. Officially, Corporatia has no interest in the planet. Unofficially, I'm certain that some hierarchs will try to find a way around the . . ."

"Sea dragons," she supplied.

". . . sea dragons' defensive capabilities." He frowned a question at her. "I thought they were crippies."

"And we used to be Cro-Magnons," she reminded him.

"Yes, well. We're still looking for five conspirators. Do you want their names?"

She shook her head, and took another sip of her drink. "I've no intention of rescuing them."

"I'm glad to know you won't get in our way. As for the sea dragons, I think they can take care of themselves; regretfully, some people will find that out the hard way." His eyes narrowed slightly. "Is there anything else you'd like to ask about the outcome of your contract before I close this off?"

"I've received my payment, so: no."

"A present, you said."

Briefly she explained to him the situation regarding Boltory. By the time she was finished, she had also drained her tumbler. After declining a refill, she said, "I can't emphasize this enough, Director: he cannot be trusted. He might kill you in your sleep. Or anyone else here."

"I have some retired SpecOps personnel who would like to do something useful with their skills now and then," he told her. "Besides, he's going to be too exhausted by the end of the day to think about anything except sleeping and, maybe, eating. The estate needs a lot of work, you know. If you're right about him, maybe he'll eventually take a little pride in building that wall, or draining that swamp. A little appreciation often goes a long way. Today a Cro-Magnon, tomorrow—who knows?"

Yoelin shot to her feet. "Butterfly," she said. "Ye gods. Of course!"

Exeter stared at her. His features hardened, as if he half-expected an attack from her. "Yoelin?" he said.

She waved him off. "Something Ellie told me. Director, you've—pardon me, but you've had women stay over. Would any of them have left behind a summery frock in my size? Anything like that?"

He dug out a Palmetto and pushed a button. Presently a pale young woman obviously engaged in cleaning something appeared in the atrium doorway. She departed after he broached his requirements, and he turned back to Yoelin, watching her as she paced around the room. "I doubt there's anything in your size," he said. "It will probably be too short."

She nodded absently at him in passing. Butterfly, she thought.

One species, two aspects, both aspects vital to the species. One woman, child and adult, inescapably and inextricably linked, one and the same. You grow beyond the caterpillar; you grow beyond the child. But you live from origin to end. Who are you, really?

Clarity smote her like a hammer.

"I'm me," she whispered, pausing at a window to part the smoke-stained curtains. She began to speak as if her words formed a mantra, a meditation. "This is my past. I can't change it, nor do I want to, now. Everything that has happened has led me to this place and time, to this moment, and to the next moment, and the next. I like what I'm doing. I'm doing some good. I like this moment. I can control it. I can choose the moments of my future. It's all me." She laughed lightly. "Butterfly. Whether it is called *Danaus chrysippus* or monarch butterfly, it's the same creature. It doesn't matter what it's called, it is. It is." She sighed. "And I am."

"Will this do?" asked Exeter.

Startled by the interruption, Yoelin whirled about, her hands already moving into defensive positions in preparation for an attack. Exeter took two quick steps back, and held a dress in front of him. It was a blue floral print on fabric grayish with age. The manner in which he was holding it suggested he was assessing his look in it, and she laughed as she held out a hand for it.

Very carefully Exeter laid the garment over her outstretched arm, and stepped back again. "I don't think I want to know what that was all about," he said. "Or do I?"

She flashed a wry grin. "Just a bit of personal resolution," she told him. "Nothing to worry about." She held up the dress. "Thanks for this. I'll return it when I'm done—."

Exeter held up a hand. "Don't bother," he said. "Yoelin?"

"Sir?"

"Until the next time."

"We'll see," she said, and departed from the atrium.

***

Dressed in the frock from Exeter, Yoelin sat on the pier down the gentle slope from the hut she had leased days earlier, when she had come to Havelox Rest to find Manohra Dhu. Stefan now leased the hut, setting it up for his comforts—so Ellie had informed her. Beside her, with half her body out of the lagoon, coiled the sea dragon, accepting an occasional piece of fruit. Shafts of early morning light from Karsh cast the surrounding woods in glow and shadow, reminding Yoelin of a summer morning long, long ago. The reminder helped; she wanted to be as she had been, those mornings as a child. It had become important to her, in ways she did not and might not ever understand.

"He's still asleep?" she asked Ellie.

Shall I awaken him now?

"Not yet."

She popped a dried date into Ellie's mouth, and received a nuzzle of gratitude against her knee. Out in the water, a fish just broke the surface, then dove back down. She tossed a chunk of fruit in its direction, and watched the tiny circles spread from where it splashed. Her adult life had been much like that—a plop here, a splash there, and concentric circles of good enveloped those around her. Some questions that had cropped up during this Rescue still lacked answers. Who was the missing Thibbony heiress Stefan had mentioned? Why had Danelle Moths been looking for her, and where was her sister Velanne now? But the answers could wait. For now, a man from her past had raised his own circles about her. That he, like herself, had been a child in that past, did not signify. He was here, and here was now. His circles enveloped her.

Yoelin's heart began to beat faster in anticipation of her encounter with Stefan. She could not be certain of his reaction when he spotted her. The events of two days earlier, when she had returned to face Runchal, had shaken him despite his experience in Special Operations. She did not doubt for a second his explanation of needing peace and quiet. One could hardly paint a masterpiece in a firestorm. And she herself was frequently in the middle of firestorms that arose as a result of her Rescue attempts.

In the long term, she and Stefan were incompatible.

And yet . . .

It is possible you are overthinking this.

Startled, she glanced at Ellie. "In what way?"

What do you feel, *Yoelin?*

"Oh, I'm going to do this, Ellie," she said. "I'm just . . . frightened."

Of?

She brushed strands of hair from the side of her face. "Oh, I don't know," she groaned. "That's the problem. What is there to fear? Don't you have unnamed fears like that?"

My greatest fear is that somewhere on the ocean floor is a drain with a cover on it, and that someone will remove the cover, and we'll all go swirling down with the water to the center of the world, where the heat will evaporate us.

Yoelin chuckled. "That cannot possibly happen, Ellie."

What a relief!

"I think I see what you just did," Yoelin said. "Thanks."

Stefan is waking now.

While Ellie slid back into the lagoon, Yoelin scrambled to her feet and dashed into the shafts of light at the periphery of the woods, where she would have a clear view of the window next to the coffee brewer . . . where she knew he would head as soon as he dressed. Already she had scouted the places where he might have caught sight of her during her childhood, and noted the angles of view and the points of concealment. Now she meant to walk them as she had then, to remind him—to jog his memory, although she doubted it needed jogging. She selected the first point, behind a large, squat tree trunk, and waited.

Inside the hut, Stefan was stirring. From thirty meters away, she saw shadows move, and smiled. So typical of Stefan, she thought. Get the coffee first. Nothing happens until there is coffee. She spotted his bare right shoulder, and knew he was standing at the end of the table. From that angle, he would have a glimpse of her movement.

She gave him that glimpse, drifting along behind random saplings dappled by morning sunlight, until she reached a small outcrop of granite. Once there, she stood on tiptoes and peered over the top of it through the sparse wildflowers.

Stefan was standing at the window!

Though she could not make out the details, she knew his eyes were huge and wondering. She imagined that the knuckles of his hands had whitened where he gripped the wood of the window sill. Even as she watched, he disappeared, and she heard a door thrust open to smack against the side of the shack. She walked further into the forest, unhurried, taking care to let the light shafts strike her now and then to tease him with her passing.

Behind her, his bare feet squeaked on dewed grass. A thump told her he had slipped and fallen. She paused in her meandering to glance back. Yes, he was regaining his feet now. He was wearing blue jeans, and his fine dark hair, as yet uncombed, reminded her of a bird's topknot. His face turned this way and that, as if he were wondering where she had gotten to. Or whether his glimpse of her had been a mirage. An hallucination, or some remnant of a waking dream.

Perhaps he will paint me as a revenant, she thought.

It was time to give him another view of her. She stepped round a clump of trees, right arm grasping a bole, and turned her gaze away from him, toward the west and the sea, as if he did not exist. For a scant two seconds she stood very still, letting him take her in. Then she slipped back behind the trees, where he could not see her, and stood waiting.

Twigs cracked under his bare feet as he approached. She could hear his breathing, raw and rapid.

He rounded the trees and stopped to stand before her, a single pace away. In lambent silence he regarded her, from head to toes and back again. He looked as if he had been posed a riddle whose solution would determine his future. She could see the answer weaving itself together in his eyes, the tumblers that unlocked a mystery falling into place. His eyes, gray with a touch of green, began to glow like pearls as the impossible shimmered into focus before him.

"Deirdre," he breathed. "You're . . . Deirdre."

Without warning, he dropped to his knees before her, and threw his arms around her thighs, pulling him to her. She felt his cheek against her belly, the warmth of his exhalation there. He trembled, holding her. She ran her fingers through his hair, and pressed him closer. Jumbled thoughts and desires ran through her like fireflies seeking to escape a jar. A light here, illumination there, she wanted him and she wanted to pose for him, anything he wanted, whenever he was ready.

"Deirdre," he whispered again. "It *is* you."

"It is me," she said, and tousled his hair.

"Oh my God." He looked up at her, bewildered. His moist eyes shone with disbelief and credulity. "How?" he cried. "*How?*"

She beamed a smile down at him. "It's a long story," she said, and pulled him back to his feet.

"It *is* you," he said again, as they began shuffling their way toward the hut. A tear plummeted down his cheek, and he thumbed it away. A light breeze pressed the frock against her, sculpting her legs.

"I suspect that subconsciously you already knew who I was," she told him. "It's why you were able to sketch me, at least with some success. Your Muse, after all."

He touched her hand, and released it, as if it were too hot, or as if he hadn't the right. She took up his hand in hers.

"I've brewed some coffee," he told her. "It should be ready by now."

"That's nice. I'll have some later."

"Later? Yes, I guess we do have a lot to talk about."

"A lot to catch up on," she agreed. "Years of it. But we don't have to do that now."

"Well . . . no, we don't." He stopped, and turned to her. "But what—?" Suddenly he brightened, his eyes clear and dry, accepting. "Oh, you want to start posing for me. Of course. And here I just bought some new canvases and oils, and a new sketch pad. Perfect."

She clasped her hands demurely before her. "Oh, I'll pose for you, if that's what you want me to do," she told him. A little grin toyed with the corners of her mouth. "But not for a painting. Not just yet."

He frowned. "Then I don't . . . I don't . . ."

She smiled.

"Oh!" he said.

"Oh, indeed," Deirdre replied, and led him toward the hut.

Check out all of the Nomadic Delirium Press titles at:
http://nomadicdeliriumpress.com/blog/shop

You can find Nomadic Delirium Press e-books at:
https://www.smashwords.com/profile/view/nomadicde
lirium

Feel free to comment on any of the stories in this
collection by visiting our blog:
http://nomadicdelirium.wordpress.com/

www.ingramcontent.com/pod-product-compliance
Lightning Source LLC
Chambersburg PA
CBHW051522170626
46811CB00002B/944